FIRE
IN THE
HEART

FAMILY TREE

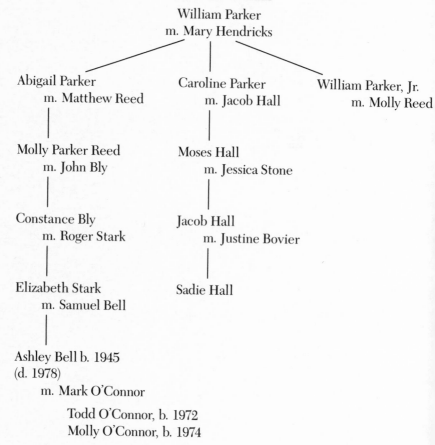

William Parker
m. Mary Hendricks

Abigail Parker
    m. Matthew Reed

Caroline Parker
    m. Jacob Hall

William Parker, Jr.
    m. Molly Reed

Molly Parker Reed
    m. John Bly

Moses Hall
    m. Jessica Stone

Constance Bly
    m. Roger Stark

Jacob Hall
    m. Justine Bovier

Elizabeth Stark
    m. Samuel Bell

Sadie Hall

Ashley Bell b. 1945
(d. 1978)
    m. Mark O'Connor

        Todd O'Connor, b. 1972
        Molly O'Connor, b. 1974

Liza Ketchum Murrow

FIRE

IN THE

HEART

Holiday House / New York

The three lines on page 243 are from "Love Minus Zero/
No Limit" by Bob Dylan. © 1965 Warner Bros. Inc. All
rights reserved. Used by permission.

Library of Congress Cataloging-in-Publication Data

Murrow, Liza Ketchum
Fire in the heart.

Summary: Fourteen-year-old Molly tries to uncover the
mystery surrounding her mother's death ten years before.
[1. Mystery and detective stories]   I. Title.
PZ7.M96713Fi   1989   [Fic]   88-45864
ISBN 0-8234-0750-0

For Katherine

FIRE
IN THE
HEART

CHAPTER 1

Molly O'Connor sat by the lake, watching ripples of light bounce on the water. The sun was low, and her friends had all gone home. Why was Dad so late? She traced letters in the sand with her fingers, then timed the pause between the waves slapping the boathouse. Finally she heard the familiar growl of her father's truck as it rattled down the road to the beach.

Molly ran up the narrow path to the gravel parking lot, her wet hair soaking the shoulders of her T-shirt. Their green pickup was parked under a tree with the motor idling. Her father was bent over the engine, scowling, his stocky frame lost beneath the hood.

"Hey, Dad, something wrong?"

Mark O'Connor emerged and leaned his full weight on the front end, rocking it up and down. "It's making a racket," he yelled. "Can't tell what it is. Slide in and give her some gas, will you?"

Molly climbed in behind the wheel, pushing aside a stack of mail. She floored the accelerator, enjoying the surge of sound as the engine roared.

"Hold up!" her father called. He disappeared under the hood again, then said, "OK—keep a steady pressure this time."

Molly held her bare foot against the ribbed gas pedal and glanced through the mail. A handwritten letter addressed to her father lay open on top. That's weird, Molly thought, some kid's sloppy handwriting on such fancy stationery. Molly knew she shouldn't read her father's mail, but she couldn't help it—her mother's name burst from the first sentence like a shout.

I'm writing about your deceased wife, Ashley O'Connor, the letter began. Molly stared. Why would someone write about her mother after all these years?

"Pay attention, will you?" her father shouted. "Floor it again!" Molly jumped and revved the accelerator, trying to read the next sentence out of the corner of her eye, but her father slammed the hood closed, hitting the dented metal with the side of his hand. "Blasted truck— now the alternator belt's loose," he said, coming to the door. "I'll fix it at home. Come on, let's get going. Move over."

Well, excuse me, Molly thought. Why are you in such a bad mood? She climbed over the gearshift and leaned against the door on the far side of the cab. Her father got in, scooped up the letter, and stuffed it into the pocket of his old canvas shirt. He gunned the truck and they hurtled up the hill so fast Molly almost hit the dashboard.

"Hey," Molly complained, grabbing for the door. She gripped the sticky tape wrapped around the broken handle and tried to focus on the warm green of early summer slipping past the windows, but all she saw were the shimmering letters of her mother's name. Molly glanced at her father. His broad hands gripped the steering wheel, and he perched on the edge of the seat as if his battered pickup were a horse, running flat-out. Something's wrong, she thought. She waited for him to start one of his Irish stories, to talk her ear off the way he often did when they were alone. But he was quiet.

Molly turned on the radio, looking for a song to drown his bad mood. What was in that letter? she wondered. When Molly's mother died in a car accident ten years ago, Molly had shut her memories up, locking them in a dark, secret place until they turned dusty and dry. Now, at fourteen, she wanted to find them again. Her father was no help; he didn't want to talk about his first wife. But questions about Molly's mother surged inside her, like hot lava long buried beneath the earth's crust. They boiled up, hot and angry, until Molly's limbs tingled and she thought she'd go crazy if she didn't let them out.

The truck thundered across the narrow bridge and up their steep driveway. In spite of her worries, Molly smiled. She'd always liked the way their old barn stood like a sentry at the top of the pasture, standing guard over the low house with its jumble of outlying sheds. They jerked to a halt and her father jumped out, still scowling. Before Molly could open her door, he was rummaging through the toolboxes attached to the truck. "Grab the groceries, will you?" he said.

Molly untangled her swimsuit and towel from the litter of blueprints behind the seat and lifted a bag of food from the truck bed. She crossed the driveway, climbed the porch steps, and set the bag on the railing, staring out across the pasture. There must be something bad in that letter, she thought. How could she find out?

"Daydreaming again?"

Molly whirled. Her brother Todd stood with his face pressed against the screen behind her. His wide shoulders nearly filled the window frame and his curly hair pushed through the wire mesh.

"I'm *thinking*. Do you mind?" Molly retorted.

"Course not. But you might bring the groceries in. I'm making dinner. Blair's still upstairs."

So what else was new? Once their stepmother went into her darkroom, she was gone for hours. Molly went in and dumped the groceries on the counter.

"Give me a hand, OK?" Todd asked.

"Sorry—Dad needs me in the barn," Molly lied. She slipped into her sneakers and ran back outside before Todd could protest.

The truck's hood was down; her father must have fixed it. Molly stood in the wide barn doorway, listening to the high-pitched whine of her father's table saw. She followed the sound down the aisle between the empty lambing pens. As she opened the shop door, the saw sliced the air, winding down to a low moan. Her father stood with his back to her, pounding a nail into a two-by-four.

"Hey, Dad!" Molly called.

Her father's hand fell in a blurred arc from shoulder to board. The nail sank, hard and firm. He gave it a final blow, then turned around.

"Hi, Mol."

"What are you doing?" Molly saw from his quick smile that his mood had changed.

"Building a new drafting table. Want to help?"

Molly glanced at his shirt pocket, but she couldn't tell if it still held the letter. "Sure," she said.

For almost an hour, Molly helped him build the table. They set screws, sanded the corners, and fit a narrow lip of wood across the bottom to keep papers from sliding off. Finally, her father cleared a space under the window and held the table steady while Molly nailed the legs to the floor.

"Good job," her father said when she was done. "Don't know where you got your patience."

Molly looked up, curious, but her father didn't explain; he was scrambling in the corner for a roll of blueprints. He tossed them onto the new table, pinned the corners to keep them flat, then turned off the light. "We'd better go in. Blair will wonder where we are."

Molly followed him out of the barn, kicking bits of straw aside with her shoe. Her father stopped under the maple tree to wait for her. "Sorry I was such a grouch, coming home." His hand was heavy on her shoulder. "We've had some problems at work." Then he grinned and Molly waited, loving the way his face broadened when he smiled. "Don't tell Blair how I drove."

"Don't worry. But listen, Dad, I'm sorry about something too."

Her father looked at her, curious, and his mustache twitched.

"I saw that letter in the truck." Molly gulped, and plunged on. "It said something about Ashley O'Connor."

Her father's eyes narrowed, the amber darkening to brown. "You shouldn't read my personal letters—"

"I couldn't help it!" Molly cried. "It was lying there open, and I saw Mommy's name—" She swallowed hard, trying not to cry. "I didn't read anything else. I swear."

"It's OK, Mol, I believe you." He ruffled her hair gently. "It's nothing important. Just something from my dark and gloomy past." He gave her a sad smile.

"Dad," she said. It seemed as if everything was quiet, waiting for her to go on. The breeze had died and the circling swallows seemed to dip toward her, as if they were listening too.

"What's up!" he asked.

"Do you think I'll look like her? When I'm older?"

He studied her face until Molly had to lower her eyes. "You look like her now," he said at last. "You're tall and thin, the way she was."

"Really?" Molly's face felt hot. She thought about the picture she'd found last spring with a date on the back: March 1978, the year her mother died. It showed a young woman with ruddy cheeks, the coloring of someone who loved being outdoors. Her hair, so blond it was almost white, fell in a long braid over her shoulder. She looked athletic and wiry.

Molly kept the picture hidden under her pillow. When she was alone, she spent hours studying it, searching for connections, but her own face, framed with lank, mousy hair, seemed pale and narrow in comparison.

Molly glanced up at her father now. He was studying the hills rising in soft ridges beyond the river.

"Dad? Why don't you want to talk about her?"

"It's too painful, Mol. I'm sorry. And it's in the past. It has to be, now that I've got Blair." He looked at her quickly, then turned away.

Molly couldn't stop; something was pushing her forward. "Dad, just tell me one thing. How did you meet Mommy?"

He hesitated, then smiled. "You don't know that story? When they built the interstate, I was working with the powder monkeys."

"Who are they?"

"The guys who do the blasting. It's a crazy way to live, blowing things up. I didn't last long. Anyway, one day we made this huge cut in the hill, dropping stones and boulders all over the place, when this beautiful woman showed up. No one knew what to make of her—she started scrambling up the mountain, stuffing pieces of stone into her pack. She'd tap on the rocks with a hammer, open them up like hard-boiled eggs." His gaze drifted over the pasture as he spoke, and his voice was quiet. "So there she was, with her long braid, her big heavy boots, and that intense look in her eyes—she came up to compliment us. Said we'd made the most perfect cut, and now she'd be able to find all the rock samples she'd need. 'Guys who build roads are heaven for geologists'—she looked right at me when she said that. After I recovered, I introduced myself."

Molly held her breath. When her father didn't say anything, she prodded, "Is that the end of the story?"

He brushed his hands to clean off the sawdust, and nodded.

"But why did she want the rocks?" Molly asked, desperate for him to go on.

"For her geology. She was getting her degree then. She could have been a fine geologist, if I'd let her."

"What do you mean?" Molly asked.

Her father shook his head. "Nothing."

Molly willed her voice to stay steady. "Dad, why did she go to California?"

This time Molly knew she'd said the wrong thing. Her father jammed his hands into his pockets before answering in a cold, controlled voice: "That's enough, Mol. I mean it. I don't want to talk about it."

Her father turned toward the house. "Let's go in," he said curtly. But Molly ran down the hill, ignoring his shouts behind her. She climbed the fence and took the shortcut through the pasture. The sheep scattered in front of her, running in clumps and bleating. Even Lotty, the orphan lamb she'd raised like a pet, skittered away in surprise.

When Molly reached the bank she slid down the path

and followed the stepping-stones out to her flat rock in the middle of the river. She sat down, hugging her knees until her heart stopped thumping.

"Hey, river," she whispered. Tears pricked her eyes until everything swirled, like the water moving at her feet.

The river answered. Other people might hear water bubbling over stones, but Molly understood the words. "Weird things are happening," she said. She skipped a stone across the pool. The river murmured.

Molly poked the tip of her sneaker into the water. She knew she should be glad her father had told her something at last. But it was like having one tiny bite of chocolate cake—it could suddenly make you crave the whole thing.

Geology, Molly thought. She picked up a flat stone and rubbed her fingers over the smooth, cold surface, then dipped it in the river. Underwater, the dull gray rock was black and iridescent.

"What was she really like?" Molly whispered. This time, the river's only answer was the steady lap of current, riding away in quick spurts under the bridge.

CHAPTER 2

Molly opened the door to the ringing of the telephone and the smell of sizzling onions.

"I'll get it!" she yelled, but Todd scooped the phone off the hook as she burst into the kitchen. He cradled the receiver against his shoulder and turned his back on her, winding the long cord casually around his waist. Molly sighed. One of *his* calls, as usual. She retreated to the porch where she pretended to look for something. Was it Andrea? No, he'd never say that much to a girl. And he's such a jerk when he talks to his friends, Molly thought. They make up their own language. As if I cared about their stupid secrets.

Todd chuckled, then let his voice drop to a stage whisper. Who was it?

Molly slipped back into the kitchen. Her old collie stretched, grunted, and let her head fall back onto her

12

scrap of rug beside the woodbox. "Hey, Crisco, you lazybones," Molly said softly. She bent to scratch the dog's ears, watching her brother out of the corner of one eye. Todd was scrubbing his rusty hair with one free hand, as if washing it beneath the pool of light overhead while he listened.

"Really?" he said. "Sounds good. Me? I'm OK." He spun around until the long cord dragged on the floor, then began to pace. "Working hard—eight hours at the lumberyard, hauling stuff around, and I'm supposed to run or bike, to keep in shape for soccer—hold on." Todd turned and glared meaningfully at his sister.

Molly sighed. "Yeah, yeah," she muttered, "you can have your privacy."

She started toward the door but froze when Todd said, "So, Kai, you coming over later? Sure, we'll be here."

Kai? Molly couldn't believe it. Kai Stewart was her best friend. Her family had a summer place down the road. Ever since school let out, Molly had been waiting for the Stewarts' car to career past her driveway, swaying under all the bikes and suitcases they lugged up from Boston for the summer. Since when did she and Todd have so much to say to each other?

Molly glared at her brother. He was laughing, winding and unwinding the cord from around his waist, spinning on one foot like a dancer. "Molly? Yeah, she's breathing down my neck. Want to talk to her?"

Molly snatched the receiver from her brother and said hello, trying to sound enthusiastic. "Hey, Kai, when'd you get here?"

"Yesterday."

As she listened to Kai's breathy voice, Molly fought a sour feeling that rose in her throat. *Yesterday?* she thought. Why didn't she call me?

"I'm only half here," Kai was saying, "the rest of me's still onstage, at our final performance. It was incredible. I've got to tell you about it."

Then Molly remembered Kai's scrawled postcard last month: "Got the lead in the school play. Yikes! I'll never learn the part. Wish me luck." Something in Kai's voice now made her wary.

"Hey, Molly, you there?" Kai asked.

"Sure. So, you're coming over?"

"Todd asked me." Kai giggled. "If you can stand it. I'm still pretty wired, you know? Listen, Mol, I have to tell you. The drama coach suggested I do something in the theater this summer. I mean, I don't want to boast or anything, but he says I have talent. So I called the Playhouse before I left home. They told me to stop by. Do you suppose I could get a job there?"

Molly heard all this as though Kai were speaking through water. "I don't know. Maybe," she said carefully, trying to keep her voice steady.

"We'll talk after dinner, OK?" Kai said good-bye quickly, and Molly stood still for a moment, her eyes burning. Everything in the kitchen—the stained wooden floor, honey-colored under shafts of light, the heavy square table with its litter of mail and catalogs, the open shelves overflowing with jars and boxes of teas—seemed jumbled and disordered, blurred. So that's how my summer's going to be, Molly thought. Messy—and complicated.

Her brother emerged from the pantry with an apple, a piece of cheese, and a muffin, and tore bites from all three. "Sounds like her play went pretty well," he said with his mouth full, nodding toward the phone.

"I guess." Molly hardly recognized her own voice, it sounded so cold and distant. "How nice you got to hear about it first."

"Hey, kid, I answered the phone."

"You could have told me it was Kai."

"Maybe she wanted to talk to me, ever think of that?" Todd picked up a plateful of ground lamb and dumped it into the pot. "Come on, Molly, we've known the Stewarts for years. Can't I talk to Kai?" When Molly didn't answer, he stirred the sauce, spattering tomato juice across the stove. "What's the matter—afraid I'll steal your best friend?"

"Shut up," Molly muttered.

"Get serious, Mol. Kai's a little young for me, don't you think? She's only fourteen."

"Nearly fifteen," Molly corrected.

"Still. I'm sixteen. There's a big difference."

So you say, Molly thought fiercely. "Next time you invite Kai over, you might ask me first," she said out loud. She took the lid off the big pot and sniffed. "You're making spaghetti *again?*"

"Got any more criticisms?" Todd retorted. "In some families, everyone helps out."

"In some families, the *mother* cooks dinner," Molly

said, mimicking his voice. She stormed out of the
kitchen into the addition, a new wing jutting square and
true against the crooked shell of their old Cape. Molly
skirted heavy panels of Sheetrock and pink tufts of
insulation as she ran up the spiral staircase into a clean,
spare studio. She stood for a moment outside the
darkroom door, breathing hard.

A small red light glowed a warning at eye level.
"Blair," she called, pressing her face to the crack in the
door, "dinner's almost ready."

"Molly!" Blair's voice was muffled. "What time is it?"

"Seven o'clock," Molly said impatiently, shifting her
feet. Water splashed gently beyond the door. "What are
you doing?"

"Developing film from yesterday. Some great shots of
the sky after the thunderstorm. I'll show you in a
minute."

Molly knew what that meant. "Minutes" stretched to
hours in that room, as though time held its breath in the
dark.

"Blair—" Molly began.

"I won't be long, I promise."

Molly drew back from the door and imagined Blair
bent over the counter, her pupils dark and enormous as
images swam slowly up out of the developing tray. She
knew how Blair's thick bangs would fall down over her
eyes, how she would stick out her lower lip and blow up
gently, stirring the hair on her forehead.

Molly tried to compare that picture with the story her
father had just told her about his first wife. Ever since

Mark O'Connor remarried five years ago, Molly had studied the quick, tiny woman who'd slipped into their home as if she'd always lived there. When she first arrived, Blair converted the downstairs bathroom into a darkroom. Molly would wait for hours outside the door, convinced the darkroom held secret passages opening into hidden kingdoms. Once, she'd even brought her toolbox in from the barn and tried to pry up the old floorboards, looking for the magic trapdoor that must lead to Blair's other life—the place Molly thought she'd been before she came to the O'Connors.

"Molly, you still there?" Blair's voice rose over the sound of running water. "If I open the door, I'll lose the film. Did you want something?"

Kai called Todd—and not me! Molly wanted to shout. Instead, she said, "Not really." She ran dizzily down the stairs, out the back door, and through the tall grass, bending low as she passed the kitchen windows. She didn't want Todd to see her.

When she reached the enormous lilac bush at the corner of the house, she stood up, panting, surprised to hear the clacking of typewriter keys. Molly crawled into the thicket of branches and hid, raising herself slowly until she could peer through the leaves into the den. Her father sat at a card table next to the window, his two forefingers pecking at his old portable. On the table beside the typewriter was the strange letter she'd seen in the truck. Molly held her breath and leaned closer to the open window.

Her father stopped typing, sighed, and yanked the

paper from the roller, tossing it into the trash. Then he stared at the letter he'd received, swore loudly, and tore it in half. Molly bit her lip to keep silent. She felt embarrassed, spying on her father this way, but she didn't dare move. She crouched low, her eyes just above the level of the sill.

Her father started to throw the letter into the trash, then changed his mind. He picked up a roll of Scotch tape, matched up the frayed edges, and taped the two halves back together. Then he folded the letter and returned it to his pocket. He snapped off the light and left the room, closing the door behind him.

Molly took a deep breath. When she was sure he was gone, she untangled herself from the bush and carefully pushed the screen door open, letting herself into the den. She tiptoed to the wastebasket, grabbed the piece of crumpled typing paper, and hurried outside, careful not to let the door slam.

Sitting in the shelter of the big maple beside the pasture, she smoothed out the paper. "There's nothing here," she whispered. Her father had typed his own address and the date, nothing else. Molly crumpled up the paper and shoved it into the back pocket of her shorts.

"Molly!" Her father's deep voice called from the front of the house.

"Coming!" She ran around to the porch. Her father was sitting on the front step, waiting for her. She started to go past him, but he grabbed her hand and pulled her down beside him.

"Sorry if our talk upset you," he said.

"It's all right," Molly mumbled. After watching him through the window, she couldn't meet his eyes.

"I didn't mean to get angry. It's just that you brought up painful memories." Then, as if eager to change the subject, he said, "Todd told me Kai's coming over."

"Yeah." Molly shrugged.

"What's the matter, Mol? Don't you want to see her?"

Molly studied the toes of her sneakers, worn from running. "I don't know," she said in a flat voice. "Kai's all worked up about joining the Playhouse this summer."

"What's wrong with that?"

Molly sighed. Dad would never understand. But he kept on talking, seeming not to notice.

"She lives in another world, Mol. And things have to change. You're both growing up."

"We're always growing up. That's what kids do," Molly snapped.

Her father laughed, throwing his head back.

"What's so funny?" Molly demanded.

"I'm sorry. I just never thought of it that way before." He put his arm around her. Molly let her head fall against his shoulder for a minute, enjoying a moment of comfort before she pulled away.

"So tell me what's going on," her father said, cocking his head and waiting.

"It's no big deal," Molly said, trying to play it down. "It's just—" Molly glanced toward the kitchen, but Todd was out of sight. "She called Todd first," Molly blurted. "He asked her over—without even checking with me."

Her father rubbed his mustache with the back of one hand. Molly realized he was trying not to grin. "Todd and Kai," he said, slipping into his Irish drawl. "Now Molly-Colleen, don't tell me you didn't see that coming."

Molly didn't feel like joking. "Kai's *my* friend. At least she was."

"And always will be. Don't worry. She has a head start on you now, but things will be different in a few years."

Molly looked down at her feet, embarrassed. So Dad noticed how her body was all long angles, like a boy's.

"Anyway," her father was saying, "Todd's got other things on his mind. And I've noticed you don't give up easily—you're fierce when you want something."

Fierce. Molly liked that. Someone fierce could hang onto a friendship, sink her teeth into it like a puppy playing tug-of-war with an old sock. Someone fierce wouldn't give up trying to find out things about her mother—just because her father wouldn't answer her questions. Molly jumped up, tossed her hair, and went into the kitchen.

Todd was draining a steaming mound of spaghetti into a colander in the sink, and Blair O'Connor stood in the doorway, squinting, her thick black hair escaping in wisps and curls from the clip at the nape of her neck.

"Hi, Blair," Molly said.

Blair yawned and peered at her family as if they were strangers. "Is dinner ready?" Blair asked. "Sorry I'm so late. The darkroom was like a drug today. Once I got going in there, I couldn't stop. I never noticed the time."

She never does, Molly thought. Why couldn't she be an ordinary, regular mother? Molly demanded silently, yanking the silverware drawer open and beginning to set the table. She glanced guiltily at Blair, as if her thoughts were audible, but her stepmother had pulled the Italian bread from the oven and was cutting it with quick, sharp slashes. The loaf's heel leaped from the counter to the floor.

"Here, Crisco." Blair snapped her fingers at the dog.

"Typical," Molly said.

"What's the matter?" Blair asked.

"You always do that," Molly said. "Make poor old Crisco clean up for you."

" 'Poor old Crisco' likes these treats," Blair said. She handed Molly a basket. "Go on, poor old Molly. You and Todd pick some lettuce, and I'll make a salad."

Todd and Molly went outside and bent over the rows of short lettuce. Shadows crept toward the garden, bringing clouds of black flies and mosquitoes.

"Stupid bugs," Todd said, slapping his neck. "Say, Mol, I'm sorry about Kai. I guess I shouldn't have invited her without asking you."

"It's not a big deal," Molly said, flicking a slug at her brother.

"Hey—cut it out!" Todd dodged and sat down in the dirt. "So I've got your permission to speak to her?"

"I guess." Molly tossed a bunch of lettuce thinnings

into the basket. Todd swiped his dirty fingers through his hair, and for a moment Molly saw a little boy's face, hiding beneath the freckles and the rusty mustache forming on his upper lip. "Say, Todd," she began cautiously, "I have to ask you something serious."

He whistled and took a deep, mocking breath. "Watch out, folks. Molly O'Connor will now be serious. Everyone gather round—" He stopped, watching the look on her face. "Sorry. What's up?"

"Tell me the truth. Do you ever think about Mommy?"

He looked away. "Sometimes. Why?"

"I just wondered." Molly watched her brother. The color deepened under his freckles.

"I try to remember her," Molly said softly, "but I can't." She closed her eyes for a minute, searching for something fluid and alive, but her memories were like ribbons, bright-colored and tangled in a wind that snatched them away before she could touch them.

"I don't remember much either," Todd admitted. He wiped his hands on his blue jeans. "We used to collect rocks together, down at the brook. She was interested in geology, I guess. I don't know, Mol." He kicked mud from his shoes. "It's no good thinking about it. She's gone, right?"

"Don't you ever wonder what we'd be like if she were here?"

Todd frowned. "Sometimes. But who knows if she'd be with us, even if she were alive?"

"What do you mean?" Molly asked sharply.

Todd slapped a mosquito. "I remember them fight-ing."

"Everyone fights," Molly said. "Blair and Dad argue."

"This was different," Todd said. "I remember once they were yelling so loud, I ran to my room and crawled under my bed."

"Really? What were they fighting about?"

"Who knows?" Todd said. "Maybe it was nothing. Even your loving brother attacks his sister." He shad-owboxed with the air just in front of Molly's nose. "Anyway, we have Blair. Come on, let's escape the bugs."

Molly followed him into the house. She thought of the set of Russian dolls her grandmother had given her years ago. You opened a big wooden doll, separating it at the waist, and inside was another, just a little smaller, and another stacked inside that one. If she kept asking questions about her mother, it could be like those dolls, Molly thought. She could keep on opening things up, but there would always be another secret inside to pry open. And what would she find at the end—an empty cavity, or a jewel?

Whatever happened, it was too soon to tell Todd about the letter, Molly decided. Maybe it was nothing. She'd keep it a secret until she knew more.

CHAPTER 3

Dinner that night was quiet. Molly found herself talking in short spurts about her lawn-mowing jobs, complaining about the Courtneys' rotten mower, until she noticed Blair studying her father's dark expression.

"Mark, you haven't said a thing since you sat down," Blair said. "What's the trouble?"

"Sorry." Molly's father took a long drink of beer, wiped the foam from his mustache, and leaned back in his chair. "We lost the bid on the Hutchins' project."

"That's terrible—I thought it was firm."

"So did we. Apparently we didn't conform to the town regulations and someone else did. Sounds fishy to me, but I guess we won't fight it."

"Wasn't that all your work for the summer?" Blair asked.

"And into the fall, too. In addition to the shops, they

24

wanted a big house, garage, guesthouse—the works."

Silence crept over the table like something alive. So it isn't just the letter that's upsetting him, Molly thought, standing to clear the plates. Or is it? She glanced quickly at Todd. Their looks joined, each one saying silently: Now what?

"There's one other thing we can try," Mark said, catching the worry in their faces. "It's not a great year for construction, but there was an ad in the paper today. I picked up the plans; it's a big one all right. The bids are due next week. If you don't mind, I'm going to spend the evening in the shop with the blueprints." He scraped his chair back and went outside, letting the door slam.

"Whew," Todd said, "that's not good, is it?"

"Something will turn up," Blair said. "It usually does."

Molly looked out the window. Tires rumbled on the wooden bridge at the foot of their driveway. A car door slammed and a girl's voice called out. Molly couldn't hear the words, but she knew the voice right away. "Kai's here to see you, Todd," she teased.

He bunched his hand in front of her nose. "Cut it out, Mol."

Blair studied their faces. "What's going on?"

"Todd's got a new *girl*friend," Molly taunted, dumping the dishes in the sink. Without waiting for his response, she ran outside, jumped off the porch, and flew down the driveway to meet Kai just above the bridge. They stood grinning at each other for a minute.

"Well," Kai said at last, "how's tricks?" She tossed her

head. Her shingled hair shone blue-black, the layers falling evenly to her collar like slate on a roof.

"You pierced your ears *again?*" Molly asked. She pushed Kai's hair back to examine a second set of earrings, tiny blue stones that glittered behind her friend's dangling hoops.

"Yeah, last month. They just stopped hurting. Want me to do yours? I know how."

"No thanks," Molly said. "I bet you'd use an old safety pin. I'd end up with gangrene."

Kai laughed, and they raced each other up the hill, dropping onto the porch swing out of breath and laughing.

"The play was incredible," Kai said.

"Yeah, so you said." Molly pushed her foot rhythmically against the floor. The swing creaked on its long chains.

"I have to admit, I loved it. All those faces out there in the dark, watching me—the drama coach says I should go to theater school. But I don't know. It was only my first time. I have to think about it."

Molly was quiet. Ever since school ended, she'd hoped Kai would be a comfort this summer. Now Molly felt foolish. Her friend obviously had other things to think about.

"You had lots of lambs this year," Kai said, watching the sheep move in and out of deep twilight at the bottom of the pasture. "Boy, it sure is nice here," she added. "I'll never forget Vermont, even when I'm starring in some Broadway show." She turned and looked at Molly, her black eyes dancing. "Just think! You can come down and see me. You'll have front-row seats, and I'll invite you backstage afterward. Sound good?"

"Sure." Molly pushed the swing harder. Kai talked as though she'd already grown up and left her behind. How did she know where they'd be in ten years? And what made her think Molly would be sitting here in Griswold, Vermont, waiting for Kai to call?

"So what did the people say at the Playhouse?" Molly asked, to change the subject.

"Just to come over when I get here," Kai said. "They didn't promise anything. Maybe they'll need ushers, someone to run errands. Who knows, there might be a walk-on part. I've got a letter from my drama teacher."

Molly couldn't think of anything worse than spending the summer inside the old barn that had become Griswold's summer theater, watching actors pace back and forth across a dark stage while the sun beckoned outside. Molly glanced at Kai. In spite of their closeness on the swing, her friend seemed further away now than when she was in Boston.

"Want to go in?" Molly asked.

"In a minute. It's peaceful here." Kai pushed the swing. "What about you? What are your plans?"

Molly hesitated a moment, wondering if she could trust her friend. "I'm hoping to find my mother this summer," she said softly.

Kai stared. "I don't get it. You mean, she isn't dead?"

"Oh, she's dead all right," Molly muttered. "That's one of the few things I know about her."

"It's strange." Kai looked at Molly as though seeing her for the first time. "It seems as though Blair's always been here—I forget she isn't your mother."

"Well, she is in a way," Molly said, careful to keep her voice low. The windows were all open behind them. "But it's weird how no one ever talks about my real mom. If I ask about her death, it seems as if they're hiding something. When people say her name, they whisper. Like us—look how we're talking!"

"Yeah." Kai spoke in a hushed tone. "It was like that at Christmas when your grandmother told that story."

"About my mom falling through the ice?" Molly remembered the way Grand Nan's face had puckered as she described the time when Molly's mother had broken through the thin ice on their pond—and the way her older cousin, Sadie, had fished Ashley out with a broom. When Grand Nan finished the story, Molly's father had left the table in a hurry, knocking over his chair and leaving an awkward silence.

"You never talk about her either," Kai said, leaning back so she could look Molly in the eye. "I always thought you didn't want to."

"I didn't know what to say," Molly explained. "But something weird happened today." In a low voice, she told Kai about the letter in her father's pocket. "Before dinner, he started to answer it. First he tore it up—then he pasted it back together. He seemed really upset. What do you think was in it?"

"Only one way to find out," Kai said.

"Read it?"

"Of course."

"But how can I get it from him?"

"Steal it," Kai said promptly. "That's what I'd do."

You're not me, Molly thought, but she considered her friend. Kai's eyes had lit with genuine interest. "Will you help me?" Molly asked.

"What—steal the letter?"

"Sure. And find out stuff."

"I guess. What does Todd think?"

"He's like Dad—he doesn't like me to bring it up."

"What about your grandmother?" Kai asked, kicking off her sandals.

"Grand Nan forgets everything," Molly complained.

"She remembered that one story. There might be more."

Molly nodded. "Yeah—maybe we could go over there tomorrow. Hey, you want to spend the night?"

"Sure. I'll call my parents."

The screen door banged open. Kai's expression changed as she jumped to her feet, knocking Molly and the swing against the back wall of the porch. "Hey, Todd!" Kai's eyes gleamed. "How're you doing?"

Todd sauntered toward them, and Molly couldn't help noticing that he'd put on a clean shirt and tried to comb his tangled curls. "Good, good," he said. "You glad to be here?"

"I guess," Kai said. She leaned back against a post, tilting her face toward Todd. Molly could imagine the drama coach whispering: *Hold it, now—wait for the effect!*

"I was ready to go somewhere else this summer," Kai said at last, "but you know how it is with parents."

"Yeah," Todd said.

Molly stood up. Vermont's not good enough for you? she wanted to ask, but instead said, "The bugs are bad. I'm going in."

Jerk, she told herself. There's only one reason Kai's here tonight. And that's your dumb brother.

For the rest of the evening, Molly put up an imaginary wall to shield herself from Kai and Todd. She watched as if they were performing beyond a glass curtain, disgusted by the way Todd's eyes followed Kai, like twin spotlights highlighting her as she moved across a stage. Molly heard conversation, but the voices came from far away, muffled by her own heart. You were dumb, her heart pulsed, beating inside her head. Dumb. Why did you tell her about the letter?

In the past, she and Kai would have run upstairs early and sprawled across Molly's bed to share secrets beneath the eaves. Tonight, the three of them played poker in the living room, and Molly felt like an outsider. It was she who jumped up to greet Mrs. Stewart when she arrived with Kai's overnight bag. As the evening wore on, Todd's voice escalated with the music blaring from the stereo, until Blair appeared in the doorway, yawning.

"Tone it down, please. I want to go to sleep."

Molly was grateful when Kai stretched and agreed. "I'm wasted, after the cast party. Let's go to bed."

Upstairs, there was little to say. Molly rolled out a pad and sleeping bag for Kai and snapped out the light to undress in the dark. "Kai," she whispered, when she was settled in bed.

"Hmm?" Kai murmured. "Sorry, Mol, but I'm gonna pass. Let's talk in the morning, OK?"

"Sure. Good night."

Molly lay still for a long time while moonlight wheeled into her room. When her friend's breathing was slow and steady, Molly reached under her pillow and pulled out a thin leather folder. She studied the photograph inside. Silver light dappled her mother's young features until they seemed to quiver with life.

"Rocks," Molly whispered. "Todd says you liked rocks. Dad says you were tall and you could have been a 'fine geologist.' But who were you?"

She waited for a reply, but an empty silence hummed above the picture. Molly slipped the folder back beneath her pillow and slid under her blanket, falling uneasily into sleep.

CHAPTER 4

Molly lay in bed watching bars of sunlight creep slowly across the faded wallpaper in her room. Saturday smells drifted up the narrow stairs and through the crack in her door: coffee brewing, bacon frying, and the unmistakable scent of her father scorching butter as he made pancakes. Molly sat up in bed and peered over the edge. Kai was still asleep; only her black hair was visible at the top of the bag, sticking up in spikes.

Molly heard a car horn, then the front door slammed. She looked out the window and saw Todd walking down the hill to catch his ride. He tossed a pancake into the air, missed it, picked it up off the driveway, and stuffed it into his mouth. *Gross*, Molly thought. But at least he's out of the way for today. Molly swung her legs over the bed and tiptoed to the dresser, pulling on her clothes before nudging Kai with one foot. "Hey, Kai, wake up."

Kai stirred and rolled over. "It can't be morning yet," she groaned. "Call me at lunchtime!" She slid deeper into the bag.

Molly looked at her hair in the mirror, wishing it would do something exotic. "Come on, I smell bacon. Let's go down."

Kai sat up, stumbled to her feet, and stood in the middle of the room, her face drugged with sleep. Molly brushed her hair, watching in the mirror as her friend dressed. Kai wore a lacy pink bra over rounded breasts, with matching bikini underwear. Molly thought of her own white cotton briefs and the tiny bra she wore simply to escape taunts in gym class. Now Kai was pulling on skintight jeans and a loose blouse. She caught Molly's eyes in the mirror and frowned.

"What are you staring at?" she muttered.

"Nothing," Molly lied. "I like your shirt. Ready?"

The two girls thumped downstairs and opened the door into the steamy warmth of the kitchen. Mark O'Connor stood at the stove, turning pancakes; Blair was pouring hot syrup from a pan into a pottery jug.

"Morning, Mr. O'Connor," Kai said.

"The queens have arisen!" Molly's father announced, waving his spatula. "Your cakes are done, Your Majesties. Be seated."

Kai grinned and pulled herself to an imperious height while her voice assumed a regal tone.

"We're charmed, kind sir," she said. "We await the

banquet." She rubbed her arms with her long fingers. Molly couldn't help noticing that Kai's coral fingernail polish matched her shirt.

Blair wiped the drips from the syrup jug and licked her fingers. "You look so pretty, Kai," she said. "But you must be cold—it's chilly this morning. Did you bring a sweater?"

"No, but that's all right. I'll raid Molly's closet." Then her eyes lit on an old sweater, thrown over the woodbox. "What about this?"

"That's Todd's," Molly said, wrinkling her nose. "It stinks of sheep."

Kai sniffed the thick wool. "And woodsmoke. I like that." She pulled it over her head and swirled around the kitchen to model it for them. "Elegant!" she said, her tiny shoulders lost in the gray-brown folds. "It's what they call the 'paper bag look.' " She folded her arms tight to her chest.

Disgusting, Molly thought. She acts like she's hugging Todd.

"Think Todd will mind?" Kai asked.

Molly's parents exchanged a quick glance. "Todd's gone to work," Molly's dad said, "so you're safe."

For a minute, Kai looked disappointed, but she brightened up when Molly's father set the pancakes on the table with a flourish. "Sit down," he said, "breakfast is ready."

As if they'd planned it ahead of time, Kai strode to the armchair where Mark O'Connor usually sat and swept his old canvas shirt off the back, tossing it to Molly.

"Here, you wear this," she said, her eyes dancing with mischief. "I'll sit in the king's seat." She pulled the chair out from the table and dropped into it, giving Molly a quick, sly look. "Put it on. Don't you like men's clothes? I wear my dad's stuff all the time. Makes him furious."

Molly slid her arms into the shirt and rolled up the cuffs to keep them out of the syrup. Her father didn't seem to notice; he slid the butter plate over to Kai and sat down with such force that the plates jumped and Molly's milk slopped onto her napkin.

"Dad!" she said fiercely. "Come on!"

"Come where?" Mark O'Connor rolled his eyes, then sat back and took a long, noisy swallow of coffee. "We going someplace?"

Molly ignored him. When he turned to make conversation with Kai, Molly took a slow careful bite, letting her upper arm drift across the shirt pocket. She felt the bulge of the letter inside, hot against her T-shirt. Molly glanced at Kai, as if to say, *Now what?* But her friend was bantering with her father, fielding his teasing about the boys in her high school with quick, sharp jabs of her own.

Molly carried her plate to the sink, slipping a piece of bacon fat into Crisco's mouth. The collie thumped her tail and licked Molly's fingers gently. Blair drained her coffee and stretched. "What have you girls got planned for today?"

Before Molly could answer, Kai said, "I'm going down to the theater. See if they need help there this summer."

"What a good idea! You going too, Mol?" Blair prodded. "It could be fun. I'm sure you could usher when the plays start."

"I don't want to be an usher. I've got my lawn-mowing jobs. Anyway, I'm going to see Grand Nan today." Molly glanced at Kai, to see if she remembered their talk about visiting her grandmother, but her friend's eyes were blank pools.

"Why not wait until later?" Blair suggested. "Go on, have fun with Kai. You haven't seen each other for months."

Molly glared at her. Couldn't Blair see this was none of her business? Kai hadn't even invited her. "I can plan my own day." When Blair looked annoyed, Molly added, "It's better if I go now. Grand Nan's more cheerful after breakfast."

Mark O'Connor laughed. "If you're lucky, she might even call you 'Molly' for a change."

"Dad, that's not fair!" Molly cried. "She can't help it if she's old. And so what if Grand Nan calls me 'Ashley.' At least she *talks* about her."

Kai stared; Blair opened her mouth and closed it. Molly's accusation seemed to hang in the sunshine that filtered across the scuffed floor. Finally Mark O'Connor cleared his throat, left the table, and poured himself a fresh mug of coffee. He stood with his back to them, staring out the window.

Kai carried her dishes to the sink. "I'm going to get my stuff together, Mol, OK?" She paused at the bottom of the stairs. "Sorry I can't go to your grandmother's today— maybe some other time."

"Sure. That's all right."

When Kai went upstairs, Molly stood behind her father, wondering if she should apologize. She decided she wouldn't, asking instead, "Dad, what are the blueprints for? The ones you brought home."

"A new development in North Conway," he said. "The biggest thing Griswold Construction's ever bid on. We're pretty nervous about it."

"North Conway, New Hampshire?" Molly asked. "Isn't that a long way from here?"

"I'm afraid so. I'd have to commute home on weekends. But we'd manage. Blair and I were talking about it before you came down." He wiped his mustache, then smiled at Molly. "You three would be fine, but I'd sure miss you."

"When would it start?" Blair asked.

"As soon as possible. It's an enormous project—a bunch of condominiums and a clubhouse for a golf course."

Blair stacked the dishes in the sink. "So you'd be gone all summer?"

"And into the fall, *if* we get it." Molly's father stared at Blair, then at Molly. "What are you two grinning about? Looks like you'd be glad to get rid of me, or something."

Molly poured herself some juice. Could he read her mind? She'd been thinking, if her father left, she could dig through his files and drawers, see if he'd kept anything of her mother's.

Blair was laughing. "Of course I don't *want* you to leave. But I must admit I'd get a lot done if you weren't here." She smiled. "Come on, Mark, don't be hurt. You know you love to hang around and talk to me when you're not working."

"I see." Tension seemed to quiver around Molly's father as he spoke. "I thought if we got this job, it would free you up a little. Give you some time outside, for once. You wouldn't have to worry about money—maybe you could even enjoy summer with the kids."

Blair's green eyes darkened. "What does that mean— that I don't spend enough time with them?"

"I didn't say that." Molly's father was pacing now, as if he were ready to bolt out the door. "But I sometimes wonder what you're doing in that darkroom. I haven't seen any giant sales lately."

Molly held herself still as Blair dried her hands slowly and hung up the towel. Her stepmother's voice was like a rubber band about to snap. "That," she said slowly, "is completely unfair. Whenever I say I'll go back to work in the camera shop, you always say no. In case you've forgotten, I did sell a cover photo last week. And the reason I'm always in there is because I love photography—and I'm good at it."

He sighed. "Of course you are. Just forget what I said, all right? Anyway, we haven't even got the job yet. With my luck recently, they'll turn us down. Then we'll really have something to worry about." He stalked out of the room without looking back.

Blair swept a mug into the sink. It caught the faucet and broke, spewing shards of pottery into the soapy water. "*Now* look what I've done!" Blair cried. She wiped her streaming eyes with a piece of paper towel. "Your father," she said vehemently, "is the most stubborn man I've ever known."

"Why'd you marry him, then?" Molly retorted.

Blair glared at her. "Because I *love* him, that's why," she snapped, and began tossing spoons and knives into the soapy water.

Molly had to laugh. "You don't have to sound so angry about it."

"You can love someone even when they make you furious," Blair said. She swiped at her bangs with a soapy hand and glanced at Molly, her green eyes narrowed to points, like jewels. "That comment you made about your mother certainly didn't help things."

Molly's face grew hot. "Tough," she said, and ran up the dark stairs to her room. She stopped in the doorway. Kai was standing in front of the mirror, contorting her face into a series of frowns, false smiles, and cool stares.

"What are you doing?" Molly asked, trying to calm down. Her heart was thumping hard.

Kai giggled. "Practicing." She pulled Molly's arm and closed the door behind her. "Now, let's open the letter."

The letter—Molly froze. In the midst of her parents' arguing, she'd forgotten all about it. She unbuttoned the flap on her father's shirt pocket and reached inside. NEVADA CITY HISTORICAL SOCIETY was printed in blue letters at the top of the cream-colored stationery. Molly sat down on the bed, smoothing the wrinkled paper. Kai leaned over her shoulder and they read together in silence, puzzling over the taped portion in the middle.

Dear Mr. O'Connor,

I'm writing about your deceased wife, Ashley O'Connor. I'm a student intern at the Nevada City Historical Society. The other day I was cleaning out files for Miss Darby, the director. I found some letters your wife had written to her a long time ago. When I showed them to Miss Darby, she told me your wife died in an accident and I should throw the letters away.

I didn't feel right about that. I thought they might have sentimental value. But maybe you'd rather not see them. I mean, would it make you feel badly after all this time? Please write and let me know what I should do.

> *Sincerely,*
>
> *Ramon Rodriguez, Student Intern*

P.S. Maybe you should write me at home. My address is: RR #3, Nevada City, California.

Molly read the letter twice, then put it carefully back in the shirt pocket, trying to keep her hands steady.

"Wait a minute," Kai whispered, "aren't you going to write him?"

Molly shook her head. "What would I say? And what if Dad's still planning to answer it?"

"So what if he does? She was your mother. You have the right."

"That's true." Molly grabbed a pencil from her bedside table, scrawled the name and address on a scrap of paper and slipped it under her pillow—remembering, too late, that her mother's picture was also underneath.

"Who's that?" Kai said quickly, pointing at the leather folder. "Your new boyfriend?"

Molly pushed Kai's hand away and sat down on the pillow, hiding everything. "I don't have a boyfriend."

Kai tried to slide her hand under the pillow, teasing. "Come on, Mol, show me. I won't tell."

Molly's face burned. "Lay off, Kai, will you?"

"Well, excuse *me*." Kai's dark eyes flashed with quick anger, and Molly flinched. When they were younger, their fights sometimes ended in weeks of silence. She couldn't bear that, not this summer.

"Promise you won't tell anyone?" Molly asked, relenting.

"Of course. You can trust me."

I wonder, Molly thought, but she stood up and handed her the picture. "It's my mom."

Kai cocked her head to the side, puzzled. "Gee, Mol, I thought—" She glanced at the faded color photograph. "I didn't know. I'm sorry." She looked at Ashley's picture, then at Molly. "She's pretty, isn't she?"

Molly nodded, near tears. "Too bad I don't take after her."

"Hey, Mol, don't talk like that. You might look like her when you're older."

Thanks a lot, Molly thought. Aloud she said, "So what

will I do? Write this guy Ramon—what kind of name is that?"

"Spanish," Kai said in a husky voice. "How romantic. He's probably gorgeous."

Molly laughed. "Is that all you think about?"

"Pretty much," Kai admitted. "What else is there?"

All the rest of life, Molly wanted to say, but she didn't. "What would I write?" Molly asked. *"Hi, I'm Molly. My friend Kai wants to know if you're a hunk? And by the way, what did my mother want?"*

"That sounds good."

"Come on, Kai. Couldn't you help me?"

"Sure, but not now. I've got to get going. Maybe later."

Kai gave the mirror a sideways glance, then turned and faced the glass, combing her hair back from her face with her fingers. She let her expression change from a sultry pout to an innocent grin. The black eyes in the mirror seemed to watch and approve the real face outside. "So, you think they'll take me at the theater?"

"I guess," Molly said. As they started downstairs, Molly put her hand on Kai's arm. "Wait," she whispered. Through the cracks in the old floorboards, she could hear her parents talking.

"Sorry," her father was saying, "that was unfair. I know your work's important."

Molly couldn't hear what Blair answered, but her father must have moved closer to the stairs, because his words came floating clearly up to them. "After my first marriage, you'd think I would have learned to keep my mouth shut," he said.

"What does that mean?" Blair demanded.

If her father replied, Molly couldn't hear him. The screen door thumped twice, then everything was quiet. When Kai and Molly went slowly down to the kitchen, steam and sunlight mingled in an empty silence.

Molly wheeled her bike out of the barn and pushed it slowly down the road as Kai chattered about the theater; should she really go alone; would they think she was weird, just a kid showing up to help out; did Molly know the names of the people who worked in the box office— as if she'd completely forgotten the letter and Molly's reaction to it. Molly was both annoyed and relieved when they reached Kai's tidy yard, half a mile away.

"Call me soon, OK?" Kai said.

"Sure. Maybe tomorrow." Molly waved, jumped on her bike, and pedaled as fast as she could up the long, winding hill to her grandmother's.

CHAPTER 5

Half an hour later, Molly was in her grandmother's kitchen, making tea. "I'm so glad you came over," Grand Nan said from her chair.

"I haven't seen you in a long time," Molly said. She set the teacups on the table and sat down beside her grandmother. Steam coiled from Grand Nan's cup and fogged her glasses. She wiped the lenses on the raveled hem of her sweater and peered at Molly across the table.

"Is school over now?"

Molly nodded, stirring sugar into the cup. "Yes, thank goodness." Molly studied her grandmother. She used to bustle from one project to the next, her short, plump fingers darting like minnows through the weeds in the garden, moving in a blur as she decorated a cake with sugar roses. Now she sat motionless, her hands still in her lap and her feet dangling an inch above the floor.

"Grand Nan?" Molly spoke softly. Her grandmother didn't move. Molly stroked the maple table where Grand Nan's constant pummeling of dough had made a smooth, shallow bowl in the wood. When did it all stop—the cookie baking, the cozy nights when Molly slept in the tiny room next to the chimney?

Molly tapped her grandmother gently on the shoulder. Grand Nan jumped, startled, but her face softened when she looked at Molly.

"Why, Molly, I forgot you were here. I was woolgathering. That's what old folks do."

"You're not old, Grand Nan," Molly protested, but they both knew it wasn't true.

Grand Nan winked. "Old enough. But we won't argue." A shadow slipped across her face, and she looked around quickly before she spoke, as if to make sure no one listened. "How old am I?" she whispered.

"Eighty, Grand Nan. Remember your party? All your friends were here. Mrs. Stone baked you a wonderful cake."

Grand Nan's eyes twinkled. "That old busybody. Thinks she owns the place, now that she lives upstairs."

Molly smiled. She knew her grandmother didn't like having a tenant over her garage, but the O'Connors didn't want her to live alone.

"Some were missing, though," her grandmother said suddenly.

"Missing from the party?" Molly was puzzled. "Oh," she said gently, understanding, "you mean my mom wasn't there. And Grandpa Sam?" When her grandmother nodded, she asked, "Grand Nan? What was my mom like when she was a little girl?"

Her grandmother turned soft gray eyes on Molly. "Ashley? It's hard for me to say. I forget so much." She frowned. "That Ashley—always running away. She never comes to see me anymore."

"She's dead." Molly's voice trembled. How could Grand Nan forget her own daughter had died?

"Of course I know that, child." Grand Nan's cheeks grew pink, and she hoisted herself to her feet, using the table for support. She fumbled briefly with the ivory buttons on her sweater, then tottered forward a little.

"Where are you going?" Molly gripped her grand-mother's arm at the elbow. It always seemed as if the old woman's tiny legs might buckle beneath the weight of her upper body.

"Up to the attic. There must be pictures of Ashley in the old albums."

Molly imagined her grandmother falling headfirst down the attic stairs. "I can find them, Grand Nan," she said quickly. "You wait here." Before her grandmother could protest, Molly ran up the stairs, down the hallway, and up the narrow second flight to the attic.

The air was thick and still under the eaves. Molly bent over the rows of boxes, reading the labels written in Grand Nan's round, even hand. "Linens; Aunt Sophie." "Silver tea service." "Mother's wedding dress."

Molly ducked her head and looked at each box until she reached the end of the attic behind the chimney. In a dusty corner were two cartons with "PHOTOS" scrawled across the lids. As Molly picked them up, she wrinkled her nose; the boxes smelled of mold. She hauled them downstairs and staggered into the kitchen beneath their weight.

"Whew! They're heavy!"

Grand Nan stirred and opened her eyes. "You found something?"

"Maybe." Molly set some albums on the table in front of her grandmother. She flipped the pages of one of them. There were pictures of Grand Nan with Grandpa Sam; pictures of Todd as a fat baby, sitting in the sandbox beside Grand Nan's flower bed; pictures of Molly on her first day of school, clutching her lunch box and biting her lip. But no pictures of Molly's mother. Now and then there were gaps, as if someone had removed pictures from the album. Turning a page, Molly noticed an empty space with a caption: "Ashley with Molly, age one."

"Grand Nan, there was a picture of Mommy and me, but someone took it out. I wonder why?"

Grand Nan started to say something, then sucked in her breath through her teeth. "I don't know. What about the other box?"

Molly opened the musty carton and laid the black books on the table. Grand Nan's gnarled hands curved over the pages as she touched the sepia-colored pictures with her fingertips.

"They're old, aren't they?" Molly asked. Leaning over

Grand Nan's shoulders, she breathed in her comforting smell. Was it warm apples? Molly had never identified the scent, but she was glad *that* hadn't changed.

They studied the photographs. Ladies in soft, close-fitting hats and shapeless jersey dresses grinned up at them; they wore beads to their knees and white stockings.

"Silly, weren't we?" Grand Nan chuckled, pointing to a young woman who sat on the edge of a table, dangling her legs and gripping a rose in her teeth.

"Who's that?" Molly asked.

"Don't you recognize your grandmother?"

"Grand Nan!" Molly laughed. "That's you? What were you doing?

"Trying to catch young Samuel, I suppose." Grand Nan flipped to the next page, where a tiny woman with a slender waist stood between two children.

"That's Mother, with Michael and me." Grand Nan sighed. "They're all gone now. So many gone." She shook her head, then pointed and laughed unexpectedly. "Look, here's my naughty friend! Lulu? No—Lucille. We cut off a little girl's braids once and threw them in the creek."

"Grand Nan!" Molly was astonished. A new picture of her grandmother was slowly emerging: a mischievous child who grew into a flirtatious woman. "How long were her braids?"

"She could sit on them." Grand Nan's eyes twinkled.

Molly grinned. "Were you always in trouble?"

"No, not always. Although Mother thought so. None of it seems too terrible now."

They closed the album and picked up another. There were pictures of Grand Nan's wedding and then, a few pages later, Molly cried, "Look, 'Ashley, age nine.' That's my mom!"

Grand Nan peered down through her glasses. "Funny little thing, wasn't she?"

Molly's mother sat proudly on a pony. She had thin, blond braids that fell to her elbows. Freckles spread across her cheeks, and she was laughing.

"Pleased with herself," Grand Nan said.

"Grand Nan," Molly said quickly, hoping to prevent her grandmother's quick slide into forgetfulness, "what was Mommy like?"

Grand Nan surprised her with a flash of memory. "A devil," she said immediately. "Always into something." She smiled, but her eyes were sad. "Let's not talk about the dead," Grand Nan said softly. "I think about death too much lately. I guess it's natural at my age."

Something cold slipped inside Molly's chest. She folded her arms and gripped her elbows. *You're not going to die, ever!* she wanted to scream, but she held it in, rocking herself gently until her stomach stopped churning.

They looked through the rest of the albums together. Grand Nan was silent, as though Molly's jostling had muddied the still, quiet pond in her grandmother's head, leaving behind a swirling curtain of forgetfulness.

When the carton was empty, Molly set aside the two albums that seemed to have more pictures of her mother's family. As she bent to put the others away, she noticed a dark envelope caught between the flaps at the bottom of the box.

"What's that?" Grand Nan asked.

Molly picked up the packet. It was small, but thick. On the outside, someone had written, in a sloping, tight script: "*Save for Ashley.*"

Molly slit the envelope eagerly. The paper was old and brittle. Inside was a leather case about four inches square. She unhooked the clasp that kept it closed and stared at an oval photograph. At first, Molly thought she was looking at a negative; white eyes stared from gray faces. But when she tipped the frame, a picture swam into focus.

"Grand Nan—look! Who are these people?" Molly held the picture close, where her grandmother could see it.

The old woman squinted. "Gracious. Are my eyes that bad? I can't see a thing."

"You have to tip it," Molly said. "Let it catch the light—there."

Grand Nan nodded. "Yes, I see now. My, what a pretty girl. I don't know who she is. Imagine, digging in her best dress—and what's that man doing?"

Molly took the frame back and cupped it in the palm of her hand. A young woman held a blunt shovel out from her body at an angle, as if the photographer had interrupted her work. The sleeves of her dark dress were rolled up to the elbow. She stared straight into the camera, her lips parted in a laugh, her eyes dancing with excitement. A man stood beside her, holding out some sort of rolled document.

Molly smiled. Something about the young woman's proud, almost defiant expression held her eyes like a magnet. "Who are you?" Molly whispered. At the angle where the photograph came into focus, Molly could see her own face reflected in the glass; the picture was printed on a mirror.

"Sadie!" Grand Nan said abruptly.

Molly stared. "This is Cousin Sadie!"

Grand Nan laughed. "No. She's a cross old lady, but she's not that old." She pursed her lips. "Sadie stole the family silver. She probably took my photos, too." She turned her face up to look at Molly. "You be careful, if you go there. Keep a tight hold on your money."

The thought of visiting her elderly cousin made Molly cringe. Everyone in town called her "Crazy Sadie." Her house was dark and spooky and she lived alone. Why would she steal from Grand Nan? It didn't make sense.

"Could I borrow these albums?" Molly asked. "I'll bring them back."

"Of course," Grand Nan said. She plucked at her skirt and looked at Molly anxiously, her eyes milky with forgetfulness. "I didn't give you a snack."

"Yes, you did. We had tea, remember?" Molly looked at the old photograph one last time. There was something familiar in that face. What was it? She folded the case and slipped it into her pocket, then gathered up a few albums. She could carry them home in her bike basket.

"Grand Nan?" she whispered. Her grandmother's eyes were slowly closing, but when Molly spoke they clicked open, like a sleeping doll brought to standing.

"I'm wide awake," Grand Nan said quickly. "Molly, you'll come back soon?"

Molly hugged her grandmother and kissed her dry cheek. "Of course, Grand Nan." Molly had a sudden lump in her throat. "I'll be back. I promise."

CHAPTER 6

Molly got up early the next morning and rode her bike all the way to the lake, plunging in as soon as the lifeguard arrived. She churned through the cold, dark water, her eyes open and unseeing. In her head, she was composing a letter to Ramon Rodriguez in California. Everything about it would be a kind of lie, but she didn't care. Her legs drove her forward as if, by swimming hard, she'd get closer to the truth about her mother. She left the lake shivering, running up the graveled path with sentences whirling inside her head, then biked to the three houses where she mowed lawns, grateful all day for the mower's roaring engine that shut out the rest of the world. Just before dinner, she grabbed paper and pencil and slipped away to the river before anyone could ask where she was going.

Sitting on her big stone, Molly wrote sentences and

crossed them out, starting over three times before she had a copy that suited her. She corrected it nervously, looking over her shoulder to make sure no one had come down the hill.

> Rock River Road
> Griswold, Vermont

Dear Ramon Rodriguez,

My father asked me to answer your letter because he's out of town. He says he'd like my mother's letters back. We'll put them in the scrapbook we made about her life. Also, did my mother ever talk to Miss Darby on the telephone? No one seems to know why my mother went to Nevada City in the first place. Does Miss Darby have any ideas?

Thank you for helping.

> Sincerely,
> Molly O'Connor, Ashley O'Connor's daughter

P.S. Do you like being a student intern? What do you do?

Molly folded the letter carefully and put it in the back pocket of her shorts. Somehow, writing a lie about her father and an imaginary scrapbook made it worse, as if she were leaving evidence someone could use against her. After dinner, she slipped outside and biked to the post office. If she mailed the letter at home, her father might open their metal box and see the lonely envelope with her round handwriting. And what if he saw Ramon's answer? Pedaling home, Molly licked her lips nervously. Dad better get that job, she thought, so he won't see Ramon's answer. The next step was visiting Sadie, but Molly didn't know if she dared go alone.

Every day that week, Kai called to report on her visits to the theater. "The director's amazing," she said one night. "She's this kooky woman with dyed orange hair and a loud New York accent. She asked me right away to be an usher. The first performance is next week—you'll have to come." Kai told Molly that she'd been to the Playhouse every day to watch rehearsals. Now the actors gave her their sandwich orders at noon, and told her where to set the props on the bare stage. "Pretty soon, they'll think I've always worked there," Kai laughed.

Molly listened, but when Kai asked what she'd been doing she said, "Oh, nothing much. Swimming. Working. Want to come over?"

"Sure. Some night when they don't have a rehearsal. I'll call you. Listen, Mol, did you answer that letter?"

"Yeah," Molly said. She was alone in the kitchen for once, but she could hear the creak of the porch swing. Todd and his friend Billy were sitting outside, drinking sodas and talking. "I can't tell you about it now. Next time you're here, OK?"

*   *   *

One morning, a week after she'd written her letter, Molly sat cross-legged on her bed, surrounded by the pictures and albums she'd brought back from her grandmother's. She opened the case holding the old photograph and tilted the glass to find the image. It seemed as if the woman in the picture had kept a mysterious secret, holding it tight for years inside the brown leather case. *Molly,* her dancing eyes seemed to say, *where have you been? I've been waiting so long to tell someone my story, and you're the only one who's wanted to listen.*

Molly set the little case to one side and picked up a snapshot of herself that she'd found in a kitchen drawer. She looked about ten years old, and was kneeling with her arms circling Crisco's ruffed neck. Molly paired this picture with the photograph of Ashley on her horse, and moved the side of her hand slowly down the stiff paper, uncovering her mother's features one at a time. First she studied her mother's high forehead, then her round eyes and thin, straight nose. Try as she would, Molly couldn't find much that matched, beyond the fact that they were both scrawny little girls. And her mother was smiling, while Molly scowled at the camera. She'd always hated having her picture taken. Just her luck that Dad would marry a woman whose camera seemed like it was permanently attached to her body.

As if she'd heard her thinking, the door flew open and Blair burst in, her arms piled high with clean laundry. "Oh, Molly! I'm sorry." She steadied the pile of clothes with her chin to keep it from toppling over. "I thought you were outside."

"You could knock," Molly said, turning the pictures over.

When Blair dumped Molly's clean shirts onto the dresser, her eyes lit on the leather case. "A daguerreotype!" she exclaimed, reaching for it. "Where did you get that?"

"From Grand Nan." Molly clutched it to her chest. "It's fragile." It would be just like Blair to break it.

"I'm not always clumsy," Blair said dryly. "Excuse me for grabbing—I love old photographs. May I look?"

Molly laid the case reluctantly in Blair's hands. Her stepmother peered closely into the glass and then turned the case over, talking quietly to herself as though Molly weren't there. "Nothing that says who it is, or when it was taken—it must have been the middle of the last century. A woman digging—and what's this man doing? He looks so official."

"May I have it back now?" Molly asked. She didn't want Blair to spoil the special feeling she had about the picture.

"Of course. I didn't know you were interested in old pictures." Blair handed her the case. "I've always felt sorry for those first photographers. They used mercury— quicksilver, they called it—to fix the image. They didn't realize it was poison."

"What happened to them?" Molly asked.

"The mercury ate away their hands. Some went mad,

or died—who's this?" Blair picked up the snapshot of Ashley on her horse.

"It's my mom," Molly said, wishing Blair would leave.

"Of course it is. How silly of me." Blair put the picture down gently on Molly's quilt. "I bet you'll be as tall and willowy as she was."

"How do you know she was tall? Did Dad tell you?" Molly watched Blair's face carefully. It must be weird for her to talk about Ashley. But Blair's eyes were as calm and steady as the lens of her camera.

"It was pretty obvious," Blair smiled. "When I married your dad, I couldn't even see the top of my head in the mirror over her dresser. We had to lower it a good six inches. Anyway, you're taller than I am already. Stand up."

Molly stood and realized with a start that Blair was right. She was looking down on the part in Blair's dark hair. Molly grinned. All last year, she'd studied her stepmother's short, wiry frame, her delicate hands and wrists, willing herself to grow taller. How had it happened, without her knowing it?

"See? You're already a good two inches above me." Blair sat on the far side of the bed and picked idly at the flaking paint on the windowsill. Her thick, dark hair fell forward, hiding her face.

"Mark tells me you've had lots of questions about your mother." Blair turned to squeeze Molly's bare foot.

Molly shifted uneasily on the bed. She couldn't say anything.

"It's natural for you to be curious about her," Blair

continued. "Is that why you've been so quiet lately?"

Molly shrugged and looked down into her lap. "Yeah, maybe." She felt her voice rise to a whine, but couldn't control it. "Blair, why won't Dad talk to me about my mom?"

Blair stood up and ran her small hands over Molly's hair, smoothing it down. "Maybe he doesn't know how."

"Well, I can't wait for him to learn!" Molly cried, pushing Blair's hands away and jumping off the bed. She stood at the end of her room, her head tilted to see out the little window under the eaves.

"Is that why you went to your grandmother's?" Blair's voice was gentle but persistent.

Molly nodded, brushing the back of her hand across her wet face.

"Did she help you?"

Molly shook her head. "Grand Nan forgets so much." She held her breath, praying Blair's questions would stop.

"If you want to keep this private, I understand," Blair said softly.

"I'd rather," Molly said, studying the tree outside her window. Then, to change the subject, she asked, "Want to look at the albums I found in Grand Nan's attic?"

She opened one of the old books. Blair sat close, looking over Molly's shoulder while she turned the pages and shared some of Grand Nan's stories. Blair laughed when Molly told her how Grand Nan had cut off the little girl's braids. Midway through the book, they came to the picture of Grand Nan sitting roguishly on the table.

"That's your grandmother in her wild days?" Blair

smiled. "Wait a minute." She reached for the daguerreotype and held it next to Grand Nan's face. "Molly—
doesn't this woman look like your grandmother?"

Molly studied the two faces: the young woman with
her shovel and the grandmother before she'd grown old.
"Not to me."

"You don't see it? Well, you know what, Molly?" Blair
was excited now. She whisked Molly's hair off her
forehead and peered into her face. "I think they both
look like you."

Molly stared. She thought of Grand Nan: short,
heavy-chested and old. Molly was tall and skinny, and it
was Todd who'd inherited their grandmother's once-red
curls.

Blair smiled. "I've always thought you had your
grandmother's eyes. So gray and still. But look at this
young woman. Don't you see yourself?"

"No." Molly shook her head.

"It's the smile, Mol. It's just like yours. Quiet, but
contagious."

Molly felt her mouth slip into a grin and Blair laughed.
"That's it—that's the one!"

Molly stood up, embarrassed. "You mean, this woman
might be an ancestor or something? I didn't think we had
any interesting ancestors—I thought they were all ordinary, like me."

Blair untangled Molly's hair at the nape of her neck.
"Dear girl, do you feel so ordinary? You don't seem so to
Mark, or me."

Molly shrugged and pulled away.

"What did your grandmother say about this picture?" Blair asked. "I don't suppose she knew who it was?"

"No. She did remember lots of other things," Molly said, feeling fierce loyalty to Grand Nan surge up inside. "She said I should talk to Cousin Sadie—that she took some photographs after my mom died." Molly frowned. "She said Sadie stole the family silver."

"*What* silver?" Blair laughed. "Those two old birds haven't spoken for years. And I bet neither one remembers why. You could go over there—who knows what you might find in that house?"

For the first time since Blair had come into her room, Molly looked her squarely in the eyes. She wants to help me, Molly thought. Why? "I don't want to go there alone—it's too creepy," she admitted.

"I don't blame you. How about Kai—would she keep you company?"

Molly shrugged. "Maybe—she's always busy."

Blair caught Molly's hand and squeezed it in her small palm. "Kai's grown up a lot, hasn't she? But you know, you two aren't as different as you think."

Now Blair sounded more like herself—trying to make hard things seem easy. Molly could never explain how unsettled she felt about Kai. She pulled away, closed the daguerreotype, and put it in the pocket of her sweatshirt, along with the leather folder that held the snapshot of her mother.

The phone rang in the kitchen, then the door opened at the foot of the stairs and her father shouted, "Molly! Phone for you! Kai!"

As Molly jumped to her feet, Blair caught her by the elbow. "Speak of the devil." She smiled. "Thanks for talking."

"That's OK," Molly said, happy to escape. She hurtled down the narrow stairway into the kitchen.

CHAPTER 7

As Molly picked up the phone, the room erupted in sound. Mark O'Connor dragged two enormous pieces of Sheetrock through the kitchen into the new room while Todd, his face streaked with sweat, yanked on the freezer door and jumped aside with a yell. Two ice trays tumbled from the compartment and sent a cascade of cubes across the tiled floor.

"Hey, Kai," Molly said, sheltering the receiver with a cupped palm.

"Molly, what's happening?" Kai cried. "Your house sounds like a high-school cafeteria!"

Molly couldn't focus. Todd stood poised in front of her, his hands cupped around dripping ice cubes. "Care for a drink, madam?" he asked.

Molly turned her back on him. "Sorry, Kai, Todd's being a jerk."

"Really? Your sweet brother?" When Molly didn't answer, Kai rattled on. "Listen, Mol, you've gotta come to the Playhouse this week. They're doing *Midsummer Night's Dream*. And they need all kinds of extras—it's going to be outside, in someone's orchard. We could be in it together. Come on, say yes."

"Maybe." Molly took a deep breath. "Kai, I need your help with something. Remember when I told you what I'd be doing this summer?" Molly turned toward the wall and hunched over the phone, hoping Todd wouldn't hear.

Kai was quiet a minute and then said, "Oh, you mean about your mother?" She sounded excited. "Hey, did that guy answer your letter?"

"Not yet." Molly was nearly whispering into the phone. "I've got to go to Cousin Sadie's—but I can't explain it now," Molly said, glancing pointedly at Todd. He had dumped ice into a glass and was filling it with a repulsive-looking pink concoction. He took a swig and smacked his lips at Molly, grinning.

"Crazy Sadie—she's still alive?" Kai asked.

"I hope so," Molly said. "I'm going this morning. Will you come with me?"

"Sure," Kai said, "if you'll go to the theater later, to try out for a part."

Molly sighed. Since when did she and Kai have to bargain with each other? "OK," she said at last. "I'll bike over in a few minutes."

When Molly said good-bye, Todd whistled and pivoted on one heel, tossing his sweatband up toward the ceiling. "Watch out, folks," he called, catching the terry-cloth circle and twirling it on his finger. "Molly's going to Crazy Sadie's!"

Molly whirled on him. "*You're* the one who's crazy. I thought we had an agreement about the phone. Whoever has a call gets time alone in the kitchen—remember?"

"I was thirsty," Todd said. "Do you mind? Whew, your face is red, red, red. Here comes that famous O'Connor temper!"

Molly raised her fist but thought better of it. For years, she'd been no match against her brother. "If I were you, I'd get someone to taste your food before you eat it," she warned.

"Hey," Mark O'Connor hauled another piece of Sheetrock in from the porch. "Calm down."

"Todd won't give me any privacy!" Molly cried. "He stands right *here*"—she pointed at an empty place on the floor near the phone—"and listens to everything I say."

"Cool it, Mol," Todd said. "Don't be so touchy."

Blair appeared in the doorway. "What's wrong?"

Mark smiled at her. "Just the usual family spats." Molly glared at him, but her father ignored her. "I've got good news," he said, brushing his hands together until a cloud of Sheetrock dust flew up from his palms. "We got the job in New Hampshire."

"Congratulations!" Blair said.

"Great, Dad," Todd said. "When do you leave?"

"Sunday, I hope. The sooner we get started, the

better. It's late in the year for this big a project." He
kissed the tip of Blair's nose, squeezed Todd's shoulder,
and tweaked Molly's hair. "I'll miss you," he said.

Molly couldn't say anything. She shifted awkwardly
from side to side.

"I thought I'd work on the new room for a while
today." Mark started to slide the Sheetrock across the
floor, glancing from Molly to Todd. "Care to help me?"

"Sure," Todd said, "but don't count on Molly. She's
got other plans." He raised his eyebrows at his sister,
challenging her. "What's at Sadie's?"

Molly glared at him. "Jerk," she muttered, "can't you
keep your mouth shut?"

"Sadie's?" Her father's eyes narrowed, although his
voice was teasing. "Better be careful, going into the
witch's lair."

"Mark!" Blair chided him. "That's no way to talk.
Sadie's not so bad. She's just a little eccentric."

" 'A little *eccentric*'? " Molly's father exploded with a
howl. "She's bananas!"

When they stopped laughing, he took a step closer to
Molly. "Seriously, do you have to go? I'd love your help
with the new room."

"Maybe this afternoon," Molly said carefully. "I'm
going to Sadie's—because Grand Nan told me I might
ask her about my ancestors." Molly swallowed, hearing
how lame her voice sounded.

"I see." Her father paced the kitchen, scuffing his
boots on the worn floor. "You don't give up, do you?"

When Molly didn't answer, he stood in front of her with his arms crossed, scowling.

"You think Sadie will talk to you about your mother? She might. But, Mol—" He stumbled over his words, as if making something up. "Sadie's an old—liar. There's no telling what she'll say." He tugged at his mustache. "Sometimes, it's best to let the past alone."

"Yeah, that's what I think," Todd blurted. "And did you ever consider how Blair might feel about this?"

Molly couldn't answer. Was everyone against her?

"It's all right with me," Blair said unexpectedly. "What harm can it do?"

"I don't like it, that's all," Molly's father said.

"Too bad!" Molly exploded. "I hate the way you hide everything—as if I'm too dumb to understand!"

Her father's face grew red, and he swore. "Don't talk to me that way, young lady—" he warned, but Molly wasn't listening. Before he could call her back, she was out the door and up on her bike, flying down the driveway to the bridge.

As Molly and Kai pedaled up Soldiers' Hill, Molly explained about her visit to Grand Nan's, the missing photos in the albums, and the way her father tried to keep her from going to Sadie's. Halfway up the long, stony grade, they stopped to catch their breath, and Molly pulled out the daguerreotype, anxious for Kai's reaction.

Her friend was only politely interested. "What's this got to do with your mother?"

"I'm not sure." Molly was suddenly shy. Kai wouldn't understand how the woman's bright eyes tugged her into the past. And what would Kai think if she knew Molly held the picture near her ear, trying to hear faint words from a distant century? Maybe she'd made a mistake, asking her friend to come.

Fifteen minutes later, the two girls parked their bikes under a tree at the end of Sadie's driveway. "Look," Molly whispered, "she's watching from the window." A white face floated like a moon across the glass, then vanished.

"She can't be that bad," Kai said, but she sounded hopeful, as though wishing Sadie might do something awful.

They climbed the sagging steps onto Sadie's porch. Everything in the yard looked worn out: an old Chevrolet poked jutting tail fins from the shed beside the house. An ancient wringer washing machine blocked the front door and a double line of sheets flapped on a sagging clothesline. Molly slipped around the washer and lifted her hand, but the door sprang open before she could knock. Sadie's tall figure loomed over them, as gaunt and weathered as the clapboards of her house.

Her sharp voice made them jump. "Yes! What is it?"

Molly gulped. "Uh, hello. Cousin Sadie? I'm Molly. Molly O'Connor."

Sadie peered down at her. She was pale and seemed startled, as though expecting someone else. "Why, so you are—Ashley's daughter. What a surprise. Now, what could you want?"

Molly swallowed. She'd forgotten how direct Cousin Sadie was. "I need to find out something—about my ancestors," she stammered, feeling foolish. "I was wondering if I could ask you—"

"Ha!" Sadie's laugh was like a cough. "Think I'm old enough to be an ancestor, do you?"

Molly gulped. How had she gotten into this? "I didn't mean—that you're that old. I thought you might have things in your attic about—the family."

"Oh? Since when is someone your age interested in the past?"

"I found an old photograph at Grand Nan's." Molly plowed ahead, although it was awkward, standing in the open screen door with Kai waiting behind her. "It might be someone in our family—I thought you might know about her."

"Really?" Sadie's voice warmed a few degrees. "Maybe I'd better take a look. Who's this?" she asked, pointing rudely at Kai.

"This is my friend, Kai—" Molly began.

"Of course," Sadie interrupted her, "the Stewart girl. Haven't seen her in years." Her voice was as dry as paper crackling. "Well, don't just stand there. Come in." She motioned them into the kitchen. In spite of the June sunshine, she had a fire going in her cookstove and the air was stifling. Molly and Kai stood in the doorway and stared.

Sadie's kitchen was like a junk shop. The counters were piled high with canning jars, old Christmas ornaments, and strange gadgets. Lead ropes for horses nestled around the paddles to an old butter churn. Odd spinning implements balanced precariously on stacks of empty tin cans. There was paper everywhere: mounds of old newspapers, torn recipes, and tattered *National Geographics* overflowed the shelves.

Had it always been this messy? Molly wondered. Or had things grown worse now that Sadie was older? The only fresh thing in the room was the smell of hot rhubarb, oozing from a pie on top of the cookstove.

"Ha!" Sadie's quick laugh startled them. "Never seen so much stuff, have you? Come on, we'll go into the parlor." She strode across the room, opened a door, and disappeared.

Kai raised her eyebrows. "This place is weird," she whispered.

Molly shook her head in warning. "Shh, Kai. Come on." They followed Sadie into a square room smelling of coffee.

"Scat!" Sadie barked. A flurry of orange, gray and tabby cats streaked past their feet. Sadie lifted piles of magazines from a sofa and set them on a table.

"Sit down," she said in a curt voice, but Molly and Kai were both looking at the massive fireplace that dominated the room. Unlike the rest of the house, the sooty opening was fairly tidy. Enormous iron kettles hung above two huge andirons. Molly could imagine her father running his hands approvingly over the wide horizontal paneling that made a frame around the fireplace. She felt guilty, thinking how she'd yelled and run off angry.

"It's like Sturbridge Village," Kai was saying, and Sadie nodded, looking almost pleased. When the old woman bent to adjust a kettle, Kai pointed to a door in the paneling beside the brickwork. "Is that an oven?" she asked.

"Smart for a flatlander, aren't you?" Sadie said. Kai's face reddened with anger, but Sadie didn't seem to care. "My grandmother used to bake there when I was a girl."

Kai pulled the oven door open and squealed when an enormous gray cat leaped out and slithered under the couch. Sadie stalked between Kai and the door, shoving her out of the way as she shut it firmly.

"Hey!" Kai exclaimed. She gripped the mantelpiece, nearly losing her balance.

"That Amos—thinks he owns the place," Sadie said, ignoring Kai's astonishment. She pointed to the cleared couch on the far side of the room. "Sit down." This time Molly obeyed and Kai followed, raising her eyebrows.

"Shall we have coffee?" Sadie asked.

Coffee? Molly was surprised; her parents never let her drink it. But she accepted the thick, muddy cup Sadie poured from an enamel pot and filled it as full as she dared with cream, adding three heaping teaspoons of sugar before taking a polite sip. She glanced at Kai. Her friend sat straight and alert, her eyes focused on Sadie. Molly realized she was memorizing every detail and mannerism. Later, she'd probably treat everyone to a perfect impersonation of the old woman.

Sadie folded her thin frame into a chair and stared at Molly until she began to feel uncomfortable. "You look so much like your mother you gave me quite a turn. For a moment, I almost thought—" But Sadie didn't finish her sentence. Instead, she set her coffee down and held out her hand. "Let's see that picture."

Molly reached into her pocket. The small folder with her mother's snapshot fell out on the floor. Molly hurriedly picked it up and shoved it into the pocket of her sweatshirt before she handed Sadie the leather case. Her cousin lifted wire-rimmed glasses from a ribbon around her neck and settled them on her nose. "So," she said accusingly, "where'd you find this?"

"Grand Nan said I could have it." Molly shifted uneasily on the couch. Sadie made her feel as if she'd stolen the picture. "She didn't know who it was."

"No, she wouldn't," Sadie said flatly. "Losing her marbles, isn't she?"

Molly was astonished. How could Sadie talk about Grand Nan that way? "Could I have it back, please?" Molly said coldly when she could control the trembling in her voice.

"Don't go all huffy on me, girl," Sadie said, standing up. "Just because your grandma and I don't see eye to eye." She studied the picture again, then threw Molly a sharp look. "There was nothing to identify these people?"

Molly shook her head. She didn't want to tell Sadie that her mother's name was on the envelope.

"There's a family resemblance around the woman's eyes," Sadie said. "No telling who she is." She closed the case and returned it to Molly. "How about the other picture?"

"That's her mother," Kai said, before Molly could answer.

Sadie snapped her fingers. "Do you always speak for your friend? It's a bad habit."

Kai's black eyes narrowed with anger but she didn't answer. The coffee churned in Molly's stomach.

"That pie must be cool now," Sadie said, taking a step toward Kai. "There's a knife beside the stove—will you cut some pieces for us?"

"I get the hint." Kai stalked from the room.

"I suppose you think I'm a mean old coot," Sadie said to Molly, closing the door behind Kai. "Some things are best kept within the family. May I?" She pointed at the pocket of Molly's sweatshirt.

Molly pulled the picture out reluctantly. "It's just an old photo of my mom. I don't know why I brought it."

"Nonsense. Of course you do." Sadie's eyes skimmed across the snapshot, focused on the daguerreotype, and then landed on Molly's face. Molly felt like an article Sadie was appraising at an auction. The old woman put a bony hand on Molly's shoulder. "I wondered if you'd ever come to see me," she said. "I expected Todd when he was younger, but maybe it's not the same for a boy."

"What do you mean?" Molly asked carefully. She stood poised on the balls of her feet, ready to bolt.

Sadie's face softened a little. "Sometimes it's best to let the past rest," she said. "But sometimes what you don't know torments you until you have to pay attention. Do you understand what I mean?"

"Sort of." Molly shifted from side to side. "I'd like to

know more about my mom," she admitted. She took a deep breath, not sure where to begin. "No one wants to talk about her."

"I'm not surprised," Sadie said, and then demanded, "Tell me how old you are."

"Fourteen." Molly waited. What did her age have to do with anything?

"I'll have to think," Sadie said. "I don't know much about you. Whether you keep secrets, for example."

"I can," Molly said, but Sadie shook her head.

"You tell the Stewart girl everything. I'm talking about something completely private." She lowered her voice, nodding toward the kitchen. "Maybe it's time you acted on your own."

Molly was stung. *It's none of your business what I do with Kai!* she wanted to cry, but she held her breath.

Sadie peered at Molly one last time, then nodded, as though she'd made some sort of decision. "Come back alone sometime," she said at last.

Molly didn't answer. She wasn't used to being bossed around this way.

Kai appeared in the doorway, looking uncomfortable, as though she didn't know what Sadie might do next. "Excuse me, Miss Hall. I can't find plates for the pie."

"Clear up the cups, girls," Sadie said, "then we'll eat." She swept past them.

"Whew! She's rude!" Kai exploded in a fierce whisper. "And crazy."

Molly took a deep breath. "I'll say." They followed the old woman into her kitchen.

CHAPTER 8

Sadie's rhubarb pie sat heavily in Molly's stomach as she pedaled down the hill behind Kai. A fierce wind whipped the bushes beside the road and turned their leaves inside out, reminding Molly of Blair's scalp when she washed her hair at the kitchen sink.

"It's going to storm!" Kai yelled over her shoulder, but Molly didn't say anything.

They biked to the Stewarts' house, where Kai changed from jeans into black pants and layers of pink and red shirts. Then Molly followed Kai to the theater and sat in the back of the barn, hoping no one could see her in the shadows beyond the footlights. Why did Kai bring me? she wondered, watching her friend run back and forth to the stage with props. Did she want to show off her new friends?

Kai crouched beside a young woman who wore her

hair in a thick braid. They whispered together, then disappeared behind the stage and came back wearing each other's clothes. Kai twitched at her silky borrowed skirt, revealing a pair of soft suede boots, folded at the ankle. The young woman had become a blond version of Kai, lost in folds of red. As if suddenly remembering that Molly was there, Kai waved, signaling her to join them. But Molly huddled in the hard seat, thinking.

She went over the little she knew about her mother's death. She was killed in a car accident, in California. Molly had always been told that the road was slippery from spring rains and mud slides; her mother's car went out of control and plunged over a bank. But why had she gone to California in the first place? And why did her father get so angry when she mentioned her mother's death?

Now Sadie seemed part of the puzzle too, the way she started to say things, then changed her mind, like an old car backing and filling. Molly shifted on the seat and pulled the daguerreotype from her pocket. She opened the case and studied the old photograph in the shadows. When someone came through the door at the back of the theater, a dim shaft of light fell across Molly's lap. She caught her breath. "What's this?" she whispered. A piece of yellow paper protruded from the soft velvet casing on the left side of the case. Molly tugged gently. As the brittle paper yielded to her fingernails, she bent close to it, hardly daring to breathe for fear it might disintegrate.

The piece of paper was long and narrow, torn from

something bigger. "There's writing on it!" Molly exclaimed, squinting at the old-fashioned script. She went to the rear of the theater and opened the door a crack. *"Receiving my deed, near the Yuba River, California, 1853."* Molly studied the picture again. A deed—was that what the man had in his hand?

"Kai!" Molly called, forgetting where she was.

Two actors, walking through their lines onstage, stood still and squinted at the dark rows of empty seats, then scowled and tried to regain their places. Molly's face burned with embarrassment. She hurried outside and waited for Kai to join her.

"You jerk!" Kai whispered, pushing her away from the door. "Don't talk when they're rehearsing!"

"I forgot," Molly said. "Look what I found inside the daguerreotype—be careful."

Kai glanced at it. "That's impossible handwriting—what does it say?"

Molly read it out loud and then said, "I'm going home."

"Now? Why?"

"I need to find out where the Yuba River is."

Kai looked worried. "Have you gone nuts? What does the Yuba River have to do with anything?"

"I don't know. It might be important. When I found this picture at Grand Nan's, it had a note on it, saying 'Save for Ashley.'"

Kai twitched her skirt. "What's wrong with you? I thought you wanted to find out about your mother. Now you're poking around with old pictures."

"Grand Nan saved it for Mommy." Molly couldn't control the shaking in her voice. "Look, I have nothing of hers, *nothing*. Can't you understand that?"

"Sorry." Kai turned away, waiting while Molly wiped her nose on the sleeve of her sweatshirt. Then she said, "What about your promise to spend the afternoon here?"

"What about it? You don't even want to be seen with me."

Kai put her hands on her hips. "*So* sorry—I didn't realize I'd have to hold your hand—you could come backstage and talk to people, instead of hiding."

Molly's eyes burned. "I thought you were my best friend," she whispered.

"What's that got to do with anything?" Kai asked. "I brought you here for the tryouts, remember? If you'd just stop thinking about yourself for a few minutes, you could have some fun."

She smiled suddenly and Molly was reminded of how quickly Kai's moods could change, like Rock River in the spring, when the ice suddenly broke open. "What's so funny?" Molly demanded.

"I couldn't believe the way you faked it at Sadie's—pretending you liked the coffee. You can act, you just don't know it. Come on, try out for a part. They need extras for fairies and nymphs. We can flit across the stage. La, la, la!" She hiked the loose skirt above her knees and leaped sideways, clicking the heels of her borrowed boots.

Molly crossed her arms and shifted impatiently from side to side. "Are you done?" she asked when Kai flopped down on the grass. "Look, I've got to go home. I know it doesn't make sense to you, but it's important to me."

Kai looked up, still out of breath. "Maybe there's a reason your dad won't tell you things."

Something cold and clammy slid across Molly, like the damp air inside a cave. "Like what?" she asked carefully.

"I don't know—I was just wondering." Kai picked at the grass, with her head down. "Since I put up with your cousin's insults this morning, couldn't you stay here for a while?"

When Molly shook her head, Kai said, "Listen, I'm sorry your mom's dead, but I wish you could think about something else. You're no fun this summer. Even Todd wonders why you want to dig up all this old stuff."

Molly glared at her friend. "I see. Now you're on Todd's side." She swiped at her tears, trying to swallow the sense of betrayal. "Maybe you'd better decide whose friend you are," Molly cried. "Or maybe you already have!" She picked up her bike, swung onto it, and pedaled away with her head down, ignoring Kai's attempts to call her back.

When Molly reached her house, everything was quiet. Her father's truck was gone, and Todd's bike had disappeared from its spot on the front porch. She went into the new room, to be sure she was alone. White panels of Sheetrock covered two walls, making the room seem bigger. An empty bucket of sticky compound—the "goop" her father used to join the seams of paneling—

stood with the lid off. His taping knives, some as big as spatulas, littered the floor. Molly decided he must have gone for another bucket.

Water gurgled in the pipes overhead. Molly knew what that meant—Blair was in her darkroom. She hurried through the kitchen and into the den, shutting the door behind her. The room had a forgotten, musty smell. She turned on a light and rummaged through stacks of books until she found a United States road atlas, opened the tall paperback, and studied the index. Running her finger down long columns of names under California, she came first to "Yuba City" and then "Yuba River, p. 32, H8." Molly's heart skipped. Someone had underlined both these locations with a red marker. She turned to the California map, then matched the coordinates. She found Yuba City first, north of Sacramento and near Nevada City—the place where Ramon Rodriguez lived. It was easy to locate the river: the same red marker had drawn a small circle around a blue squiggling line that branched quickly into the North, Middle, and South Forks of the Yuba. Just north of the circle, black arrows pointed to Nevada City and a town called Allegheny.

Molly shook her head. Did her mother make these marks? The atlas was an old one; some of the pages were torn. Anyone could have looked up Yuba River. Maybe it wasn't Ashley. But if it was, why were these places important to her? And Ramon Rodriguez had written from Nevada City . . .

Molly looked around quickly, then opened the deep

drawer in her father's desk. The files inside were jumbled and overflowing, but the folders were in rough alphabetical order. Molly saw her own name somewhere in the middle, but she was more interested in a file, jammed against the front of the drawer, that said, "Ashley."

Molly pulled it out with trembling fingers and opened it. The folder was empty. *"Why?"* Molly whispered. "It's like you want to erase her life. Why are you *doing* that?"

An engine grumbled on the hill; her father's truck passed the windows of the den and skidded to a stop in front of the house. Molly shoved the file back into the drawer and went outside, snaking her way down the pasture to the river with the map book rolled into a thick tube under her arm.

Molly's father spent Sunday packing his truck while the rest of the family hovered nearby. After lunch, Todd took his bike apart and littered the barn floor with sprockets, gears, and wheels. Molly went into the pasture to see Lotty, the orphan sheep she had raised, then climbed a tree that arched over the river. She sat and stared at the water. Her fight with Kai, and all the unanswered questions about her mother, sat like heavy stones in her belly.

At four o'clock, her father closed the long toolboxes that were built into the back of his truck and tossed his duffel bag into the cab. Molly waited on the porch steps while Blair and Todd said their good-byes. She came over reluctantly when her father beckoned.

"Cut the long face, Molly-Colleen," he said. "I'll be home Friday. You might even like having me gone."

"My name is *Molly*."

Her father cupped her chin in his calloused hand. "Sorry, Mol," he said. "The shop's all yours if you feel like making something while I'm away." He kissed her forehead; Molly felt the soft tickle of his mustache.

"OK, Dad. Good-bye." Molly watched the pickup rattle down the driveway, spewing stones from its wide tires. When the truck crossed the bridge, she turned around. Todd was already kneeling beside his bike, and Blair stood with her feet planted in the grass, crumpling a tissue. Tiny shreds of paper floated to the ground.

"Blair—what are you doing?" Molly demanded.

Blair started guiltily and then stooped to pick the bits of paper from the grass. "Just thinking." She smiled. "I'm going to the darkroom now. Shall we fix dinner in an hour or so? Todd?"

Todd was scrubbing his bike chain with an old rag. "The Stewarts asked me over," he said without looking up. "We might go to a movie after supper." He glanced at Molly. "Kai said you're not speaking. What happened?"

"None of your business." Molly turned and walked away as casually as she could. Upstairs in her room, she lay across the bed, looking out her low window into the maple tree. The string of an old bird feeder dangled from a branch below; Molly wished she were small enough to swing out from her windowsill, shinny down the cord and into the hole where the squirrels lived. She would hide there until this whole miserable summer was over.

"Molly?" Blair poked her head around the doorway and plunked herself down on the bed, her green eyes full of concern. "What's gone wrong? Things aren't working out between you and Kai?"

"We had a fight."

"Want to talk about it?"

"Not really." Molly couldn't bear to tell anyone about the feeling of betrayal that had been added to the other hurts inside.

"Why don't you call her? Someone has to be the first one to break the ice. It's hard, I know," Blair said, picking at the rumpled bedspread. "I hate apologizing to Mark after we've been angry with each other."

Molly rolled over and faced the window again. She didn't want to think about Blair arguing with her father. Things were confusing enough already.

Blair stood up suddenly, bumping her head on the low ceiling. "Ouch!" she exclaimed, rubbing her scalp. "I always forget about your roof." She tugged at Molly's foot, hanging over the side of the bed. "What happened at Sadie's? Find out anything interesting?"

Molly fixed her eyes on a tall pine tree, its crown towering above the ridge beyond the river. "No," she said, keeping her voice steady.

"Molly!" Blair exclaimed, exasperated. "Look at me!"

Molly twisted her head at an awkward angle. Blair stood with her hands on her hips, her eyes flashing.

"What's wrong?" Molly asked.

Blair threw up her hands. "Never mind. I give up. I'll never get past your stone wall, no matter how hard I try."

"Could you close the door, please?" Molly called, but Blair was gone. *What's she ranting about now?* Molly wondered.

The phone rang downstairs. Todd answered it and called, "Molly! Phone!"

Molly lay still and covered her ears, ignoring Todd's shouts.

Todd spoke into the phone again, then hung up; and ran upstairs. As he passed Molly's room he stopped. "What the—I thought you were outside. Didn't you hear me calling you?"

"Yes."

"So what's the deal? You don't want to talk to anyone?" When Molly didn't answer, Todd leaned against the doorframe. "Well, in case it interests you, that was Kai. She was calling to invite you to the movies."

"Thanks, but no thanks."

Todd paced up and down in her room, slapping his open palms rhythmically against his thighs. "Why not? It's not like a date or anything. Her *parents* are coming, if you can believe it."

"I'm *so* happy for you. Now will you please get out? You take up too much space in here." Molly sat up on her bed and glared at her brother. Her small bedroom always felt more crowded when Todd was in it, and just now he reminded her of a bear, with his arms dangling from his thick shoulders and his worn sneakers pushing her rag carpet from side to side.

"How much space would you like me to take?" Todd asked.

"None would be good," Molly said. "And you look just like Dad when you scowl." She rolled over and turned toward the window again. "Please close the door."

"You're turning into a loner. You know that?" Todd said to her back. When Molly didn't answer, he stalked out, leaving the door wide open.

A cold emptiness crept from Molly's feet up into her belly. She jumped up, slammed her door, and sat with her back against it, listening to water run in the shower. Todd whistled, then his bare feet slapped along the hall. Molly focused on each sound: the banging of drawers, Todd's closet door closing, then his feet passing her door again as he ran downstairs. From her window, Molly watched Todd pedal down the driveway on their father's bike.

Now's my chance, she thought. She pulled her windbreaker over her head, went outside for her bike, and coasted down the driveway, ignoring the dark clouds gathering over the hills.

CHAPTER 9

This time, the ride up Soldiers' Hill to Sadie's seemed endless. By the time Molly reached her cousin's driveway, her legs ached and it had started to rain. She parked her bike under a tree and stood still for a moment in the shelter of the branches, watching the house. The sheets were gone from the line and the doors of the shed yawned open, revealing an empty stall where Sadie parked her old brown Chevy.

Molly ran up onto the porch and knocked on the door. Nothing happened. She stepped into the kitchen and called softly, "Cousin Sadie?" The house creaked. Rain spattered on the windowsills and a pair of thin curtains sighed gently in the wind.

"Cousin Sadie?" Molly called again. A sharp thud in the living room made her heart pound until she saw the

lopsided head of Amos, the cat, appear in the doorway.
He stalked in a wary circle around Molly's feet.

"Amos, where's Sadie?" Molly whispered, bending to
scratch the cat behind one chewed-up ear. She stood up
suddenly, remembering the scene in Sadie's parlor: Kai
reaching for the handle on the oven door, Amos jumping
out, and Sadie pushing Kai away. Sadie didn't want Kai
to look in the oven, Molly thought. Why?

She hurried into the parlor, looking behind her with
every step. Her heart racing, she opened the bake oven,
holding her breath against the sickly smell of cat urine.
Inside was a huge curved chamber, rising to a dome like
an enormous loaf of bread. A torn section of blanket was
balled up at the front; Molly guessed this was where
Amos slept. She turned on a standing lamp and pulled it
closer to the fireplace. At the back was a small, flat box,
tied with string. A faded label on one end said: *"Ashley."*

Molly didn't even think. She grabbed the box, broke
the string, and lifted the lid. It was filled with black-
and-white photographs, and Molly recognized her mother's face immediately. There were baby pictures,
snapshots of her mother learning to climb stairs, photographs of Ashley as a teenager, with her hair long and
wild and her eyes gazing away from the camera.

Molly heard a motor. Through the window, she saw
Sadie's car lurch slowly into the driveway, taking the
sharp turn like an elephant. Feeling desperate, Molly
unzipped her windbreaker, yanked it over her head, and
wrapped it quickly around the box. She was waiting in

the kitchen, trying to hold it casually, when the old woman climbed the steps.

"So," Sadie said approvingly, "you came sooner than I thought. Been here long?"

"I just arrived," Molly lied, trying to stay calm.

Sadie hung her coat on a hook in the kitchen, and then beckoned to Molly. "Let's go into the parlor. We can talk there."

Molly hesitated in the doorway, ready to bolt. In her haste, she'd forgotten to close the oven door, and she'd left the light on. She clutched her windbreaker while Sadie looked in the oven. The old woman turned to give her a cold stare, then gripped Molly's shoulder with a gnarled hand. The box of photographs tumbled to the floor.

"If there's one thing I hate, it's a thief," Sadie said. "Give that back to me."

Molly picked up the box, backing away from the old woman. "These are my mother's pictures," she said. "You stole them."

"*I stole them*," Sadie mocked. "And just what do you think you're doing?"

"They're mine!" Molly cried. "And Todd's! You can't keep them here."

"Not so fast." Sadie shut the door behind Molly and pointed at the couch. "Sit down."

Molly shook her head. "You can't boss me around. I can leave if I want."

"True. And I can tell you some things, if I want. Or you can go on wondering why no one talks about your mother." Sadie sat down in her chair and waited for a long moment. Molly was motionless, listening to the rain drip steadily from the eaves onto the bushes outside. When she finally settled on the edge of the couch, Sadie leaned her head back against the chair and closed her eyes. "Go ahead and open it," she said.

"I already did," Molly said coldly. Sadie didn't move. "You took these from Grand Nan's albums," Molly added, knowing it was true. "Why?"

Sadie stood up and went to the window. Her bony shoulder blades showed through the thin wool of her sweater. "Your mama was my friend, believe it or not," she said. Her voice was so scratchy and quiet, Molly had to lean forward to hear her. "When Ashley was your age, she used to visit me. She talked about running away from your grandparents. Said they didn't understand her."

Molly was shocked. She thought of all the times she'd escaped from her own house to be with Grand Nan and Grandpa Sam, when he was still alive. How could anyone leave *them* to go to Sadie's?

"They were just like anyone else's parents," Sadie said, as if reading her thoughts. "Perfectly fine, unless you're a teenager and have to live with them. Surely you understand that." All the energy had drained from her voice. She sounded old and tired. "Your mom was like an adopted girl to me sometimes. She didn't mind my ornery streak, just laughed and told me to cheer up. And I did, often enough." She coughed. "When she died, it was like the sun disappeared. I had nothing to help me remember her—and I thought your grandmother wouldn't miss the pictures. She's been someplace else the last few years."

Molly shifted uncomfortably on the couch. "It's still not fair of you to keep them," she said. Her voice trembled. "Everyone's taken my mother away from me, until I have nothing left. They won't even talk about her death."

Sadie turned around. The rims of her eyes were raw with unspilled tears. "You're like her, you know."

"How?" Molly asked in spite of herself.

"Stubborn—and proud. Brave, too." Sadie sighed. "I guess you'd better come upstairs. I've got something to show you."

They went through the kitchen and up a narrow stairway. Sadie was slow; one of her legs didn't bend at the knee and she had to hoist it at each step, as though dragging a slow child behind her.

At the top of the stairs was a dingy, cluttered bedroom. Sadie's house was a low Cape; the ceiling nearly touched the floor beneath the eaves. Rain teemed on the slate roof overhead and a steady drip fell into a bucket beneath the window.

"Roof leaks," Sadie said shortly, "and I'm too old for ladders."

This was the first time Molly had heard Sadie admit to her age. She thought of Grand Nan, who was cheerfully blunt about her aches and pains. It was clear Sadie never asked anyone for help. Molly felt a strange tug inside her. She looked more closely at how shabby things were:

the torn curtains, the carpet worn to the nap, the elbow patches on Sadie's faded sweater. She's poor, Molly thought. Did that make her cross?

Sadie was opening a bureau drawer, tugging on the glass knobs. "Nope!" she said, peering inside. "Wrong one." As she wrestled to close it, Molly stared. A jumble of baby shoes lay on the bottom: white, blue, and pink boots; leather moccasins; knitted booties. Sadie shut the drawer without comment and Molly sensed, from the old woman's fixed expression, that she shouldn't ask questions.

"These are my files." Sadie opened the next drawer and sifted through a pile of yellowed newspaper clippings until she came to a long envelope, sealed with brittle tape. "Here it is," she said, reading the scrawled handwriting on the outside. She handed it to Molly. "I guess you're old enough to handle this. But read it at home. I don't like tears." She paused, then added, "If I were you, I wouldn't discuss this with your father."

Molly studied the inscription on the envelope: "California, spring 1978." In 1978, she'd been four years old. 1978 was the year her mother died.

She followed Sadie slowly downstairs, her fingers itching to open the envelope. She glanced toward the parlor. "What about the pictures?" she asked.

Sadie cleared her throat. "Make me an offer."

Molly forced herself to look up into Sadie's sharp eyes. "If I gave them to Blair, she could print up some copies. Then there'd be pictures for all of us—Todd, too."

Sadie's mouth straightened into something like a

smile. "All right." Molly put on her windbreaker, and Sadie covered the box with a plastic bag. "Look, the rain's stopped. Run along before you get wet."

Molly zipped the envelope into the deep pocket of her jacket, then looked into the old woman's weathered face. She took a deep breath. "Sorry I was snooping."

This time, Sadie's lips actually turned up a little. "I guess you're right—I did the same thing years ago, snitching things from your Grand Nan's attic."

Molly smiled too. "Thanks for the pictures—and for this." She pointed to her pocket.

Sadie's face lost its pallor. "Don't thank me yet. Come back if you want to talk. I don't have a phone—but I'm almost always here." She dismissed Molly with a wave of her hand.

Molly put the box in her bike basket and pedaled furiously down Soldiers' Hill, gulping in the fresh, wet air. The envelope in her jacket burned with its hidden secret, driving her legs forward like pistons in an engine.

CHAPTER 10

Molly went straight to her father's shop in the barn and closed the door behind her. The sky was clearing; soft evening light poured in through the dusty window. Molly set the box of pictures on the drafting table, took off her jacket, and pulled out the envelope. Inside were two yellowed clippings, from a paper called *The Daily Gazette*. The first was dated March 25, 1978.

MUDSLIDE ON ROUTE 49 CLAIMS TWO LIVES, the headline read. Molly sat down on her father's stool and spread the clippings on the table. She blinked as each word leaped out, stinging her eyes.

> *On Monday night, Michael Smith of Allegheny was driving home along the South Fork of the Yuba River when he discovered a pickup truck overturned in a ravine. Smith drove to*

the nearest house and notified the police. Rescue workers were on the scene for at least two hours before they were able to free the victims, a man and a woman who were pronounced dead on arrival at the County Hospital.

The victims were identified as Paul Leone, from the Branch Road outside Nevada City, and Ashley O'Connor, of Griswold, Vermont.

Police Sergeant Donovan reported that Route 49 was slick following heavy spring rains, and that occasional mud slides made driving treacherous. After studying the skid marks, Donovan guessed the driver lost control, spun around, and plunged into the ravine.

There is no guardrail on that section of the highway, although local residents have often complained about the hairpin turns leading into their mountainous community.

When Molly finished the first clipping, she was crying. The words seemed to slide across the paper; she read the second article through tears, feeling a deep, cutting pain inside.

QUESTIONS ABOUT YUBA RIVER CRASH PERSIST, the next headline read. The article, dated March 27, 1978, continued:

An unidentified rental car, left in front of Glazer's Inn in Nevada City, has been identified as one rented to Ashley O'Connor, a victim in Monday's fatal crash. The car was a blue Ford sedan, rented by Ms. O'Connor at the Sacramento airport.

According to an anonymous source, Ms. O'Connor was registered at Glazer's Inn, but spent much of the weekend camping in the Allegheny area.

It's not clear how or when she linked up with Leone. Nevada City residents interviewed by this reporter were curious about Leone's activities. "It's not like Paul to run off with someone from out of town," said a neighbor. "Especially during a storm, when police asked people to stay off the roads."

In a brief telephone interview, Ms. O'Connor's husband, Mark O'Connor, of Griswold, Vermont, told this reporter that the victim had made the trip in order to do geological research, and that he had never heard her mention Mr. Leone.

Police are investigating the accident. Any persons with information about Ms. O'Connor or Mr. Leone's activities during the weekend are encouraged to call the Police Department.

There was a third piece of paper; Molly recognized her mother's obituary, which she'd read before. She stuffed everything back into the envelope and sank to the floor of the shop, where she cried until her throat ached. She felt as if someone had taken her few pictures and memories of her mother and ground them into the dirt with the heels of his muddy boots. Molly's head was spinning. She stood up, shivering with sobs. Her father's canvas shirt was hanging on the hook behind the door; she put it over her T-shirt.

"Dad, please come home," Molly whispered, huddling her face into the shirt collar. It smelled like her father: the sweet scent of raw wood mixed with the smell of polyurethane. "Was she in love with someone else? How could Mommy do that to you?"

Molly began to pace up and down in front of the window, shaking her head and rubbing her eyes. Until this moment, she'd never pictured her mother's death. Now, she could see a truck squealing out of control, a stranger's hands clutching the wheel, the truck plunging into the ravine, and the horrified faces as trees rose up to meet the windshield. Molly plugged her ears, but the roaring inside her head escalated until she heard a ragged scream that she thought was her mother's desperate cry for help. But it was her own shrill voice.

"You stupid idiot!" Molly raged, accusing her mother. She picked up a piece of scrap wood and hurled it at the wall. It missed, shattering the window over her father's worktable. Glass fell in a cold, tinkling cascade, littering the shop floor.

Molly held her breath, listening to the empty silence that followed. Then she ran outside and down the hill, taking the long route through the pasture, out of sight of the house. When she reached the riverbank, she hurried upstream along a beaten deer trail until she came to a hemlock ravine, where the branches made a graceful arch across the river. Molly threw herself down on the ground, buried her face in the soft pine needles, and sobbed.

"How did she meet this man?" Molly cried out loud. "Who was he?" She remembered her father saying to Blair—it seemed like months ago, now—"After my first marriage, you'd think I would have learned."

And then, as if someone had knocked the breath out of her, Molly sat up, gasping. *"Yuba River,"* she breathed. The name on the piece of paper inside the daguerreotype. The river that was underlined in the atlas. Her mother's accident happened on a fork of the Yuba River. Molly felt lost in something too big to understand. She heard Sadie's dry voice, crackling as clearly as if she stood beside her, saying, "Don't thank me yet."

Molly shook as if she had a fever. "I HATE YOU!" she screamed, pounding the ground with her fists. She hated Sadie for giving her the article, hated her mother for doing something so stupid—and hated herself for asking the questions that opened up the Russian dolls, one by one, revealing an ugly secret inside.

From the top of a pine tree, a white-throated sparrow threw its high, piercing song to the purple sky. Sometimes, that six-note call was comforting. But tonight it was the most lonesome sound in the world. Molly stood up and made her way slowly along the rough trail that cut through the woods to Grand Nan's.

*   *   *

When she reached her grandmother's, she found the old woman out beneath her window boxes, snipping dead leaves from her geraniums. The sight of Grand Nan, with her oversized glasses, faded apron, and thick, wrinkled stockings, brought Molly to a standstill. "Hey, Grand Nan," she called softly.

Her grandmother turned and waved, but her wrinkled cheeks sagged into a frown when she saw Molly's face. "Why, Molly, what's wrong?"

Molly ran to her grandmother and put her arms around her.

Grand Nan gently patted her back. "There, there," she said soothingly, "someone hurt your feelings?"

Molly nodded, unable to speak.

"Let's get away from these dratted mosquitoes," Grand Nan said. Molly followed her numbly into the screened porch that had once been a summer kitchen. The room smelled of roses; an enormous bouquet of June blossoms filled a pitcher on top of the unused, rusty cookstove. Grand Nan's knitting sprawled in a bundle on the couch. "I live out here, now that it's warm," she said. She drew Molly down beside her and rubbed Molly's hands between her own dry palms. "Tell me what happened."

"I went to Sadie's, just like you told me—" Molly blurted.

"Did I send you there?" Grand Nan interrupted. "What a silly thing for me to do. That old coot—she's enough to make anyone cry."

Molly tried to smile. "Grand Nan, you were right. Sadie did take some of Mommy's things." Her grandmother looked puzzled and Molly knew she'd forgotten the whole incident. Suddenly, she felt impatient. "I came to see you about Mommy, remember?"

Grand Nan's gray eyes seemed to lose their color. "Did you, Molly? I'm afraid I've forgotten. What happened?"

"Sadie gave me something—" Molly started to explain, then stopped. Her grandmother wouldn't understand. And what if she didn't know about the man in the truck? Wouldn't it be cruel to tell her?

It was so hard to be patient, Molly thought. For the last year, as her grandmother's memory began to fade, Molly felt as though she had lost Grand Nan in some dark, wet cave full of branching tunnels. *It isn't fair!* a silent voice cried inside. *She's supposed to be the grown-up, the one who remembers everything—not me.*

Molly leaned against her grandmother's shoulder, wishing she were small enough to climb into her lap again and hear the stories Grand Nan used to tell her.

"Grand Nan," Molly said, looking up. Her grandmother's chin was quivering. "Grand Nan, don't worry. It doesn't matter. Tell me a story about Ashley and me. When I was little." She snuggled close to Grand Nan's plump side. Maybe her grandmother could bring back the other Ashley, the one who loved Molly and Todd, the one Molly had tried to find the last few weeks.

"Well, let's see." Grand Nan was quiet a moment, then she smiled. "I don't believe she ever knew you were little," Grand Nan said. "She talked to you as if you understood everything. I remember once, I walked into your kitchen. You were sitting in your high chair, your chin all red from eating beets, and your mother was holding up two rocks, telling you their names with big scientific words, as if you knew what they meant." Grand Nan chuckled. "And you just opened your mouth and pounded on the tray with your spoon, yelling 'More beet! More beet!' You didn't care about the rocks."

"So she was a geologist," Molly said when they had stopped laughing.

"Why, that's right!" Grand Nan placed the fingertips of one hand gently against her forehead and closed her eyes. "Someone sifts sand all over my brain," she said softly. "It feels like talcum powder in there, sometimes."

Molly held her breath. *Please* remember something, she begged silently.

"We lost her to that geology," Grand Nan said at last. "Her father was dead set against it, but she never fit in here, growing up. She was gone too soon. Gone away to school; gone in the summers, driving along the big roads." Her grandmother's voice rose and fell in a soft rhythm, and her face shone for a minute, lit by memory. "You know, she said she could read the history of the earth in those cuts they made with dynamite."

"Yeah, Dad told me."

Molly waited. Grand Nan was quiet again, looking out through the screened walls into the moving shade. A long branch rubbed against the roof of the screened porch. "It's a wonder she came back at all," Grand Nan said finally. "She was so set on her studies. But one of those times, out on the road, she met your father. All of a sudden they were home, buying that old house, fixing it up, having a family."

"Why did she go out west?" Molly asked at last.

Her grandmother cocked her head to one side and pulled back, blinking. "I don't know." Grand Nan's pale eyes filled slowly and tears collected on the lower rims of her glasses. "Maybe she still had the wanderlust. Your father tried to hold her—but none of us could."

"But what was in California?" Molly persisted.

Grand Nan shook her head. "It's terrible, when your memory's gone."

"I know," Molly said. "I know." It was her turn to comfort her grandmother. She put her arms around the old woman's soft waist.

They held each other tight for a few minutes. Then Grand Nan wiped her glasses on the hem of her apron and pulled herself up out of the deep cushions. "Did you come for a snack?" she asked.

Molly nodded. And comfort, she thought to herself.

"How about some cookies? That old busybody who lives upstairs—what's her name?"

"Mrs. Stone?" Molly smiled. Grand Nan always complained about the hot meal Mrs. Stone fixed for her every day—but Molly knew she secretly enjoyed it.

"Yes, that one. She made me some sugar cookies. Would you like some? And a glass of milk."

"Sounds great. Want me to help you?"

"No thanks. You stay right there." Grand Nan walked

away slowly and Molly curled into a ball on the couch, closing her eyes and pretending she was still young enough to be waited on. She thought of the stories Grand Nan had told her, and all at once, as if a great wind had thrown open the doors on an empty barn, a golden memory rushed over Molly, a memory that clashed with the images roused by the newspaper.

She saw herself, a little girl with bare, chubby legs, crouched beside the river. Her mother, a young woman with fine, silky hair, her legs braced in deep water, was heaving rocks across the current, making a crude dam. Behind Molly, someone—her grandmother perhaps?—spoke in a slightly scolding tone. Molly's mother shook her head at the older woman, as if to say: Don't worry. She's all right. Then, slipping toward her daughter, a splash of silver droplets catching the sunlight, Ashley held out long, wiry arms, her smile beckoning. And Molly, a laugh bursting from her throat, leaped across the icy water into her mother's embrace.

CHAPTER 11

Molly woke to a feeling of wet sandpaper rasping against her cheek. She rolled over, bumping her head against Crisco's long snout. The old dog was licking her face.

"Crisco, stop! Where am I?" Molly stood up stiffly. The sweet smell of roses and a gentle rustle of leaves brought her back to Grand Nan's screened porch. An evening chill had fallen over the outdoor room, and it was nearly dark. Molly followed the white plume of Crisco's tail through the pantry shed, drawn to the soft, distant light like the June bugs rattling insistently on the screens. Her grandmother sat in her kitchen rocker watching television, and she jumped, startled, when Molly stumbled in.

"Goodness, child! I thought you'd gone. What was I

thinking about? When I let Crisco in, I never thought she was looking for you!"

Molly yawned and rubbed her eyes. "I must have been asleep a long time. Does Blair know I'm here?"

Grand Nan blushed and lowered her eyes, like a small child who has done something wrong. "She called—but I'm afraid I told her you'd left. I'm sorry," Grand Nan added in a whisper.

"That's OK. I'll call her now." Molly dialed her number, letting the phone ring on and on. She stared numbly at the flickering television screen, then set the phone down, forcing her brain to wake up. "No answer. I guess I'd better walk home," she said.

Grand Nan gave her a worried look. "In the dark? Is that safe?"

"I'll borrow your flashlight."

"That's all right, then." Grand Nan's eyes had already strayed back to the television.

Molly kissed her forehead. "Night, Grand Nan. Enjoy your program."

She walked home along the road, the flashlight slashing paths through the tall weeds growing in the ditches. Crisco padded along beside her, breathing heavily. When they got closer to the bridge, Molly saw a round ball of light bobbing unevenly, suspended in the dusk from an invisible hand. Blair was shouting her name above the soft riffles of the river.

"Blair! I'm here!" Molly jogged toward the bridge. What could she tell her stepmother? The flashlight's beam caught Molly's face and held steady a moment;

Molly shielded her eyes with her hand as Blair hurried toward her.

"Molly! Where were you? I was worried sick—I called the Stewarts, and your grandmother—" Blair groped for Molly, clutching her arm at the elbow. Her voice was thick, as if she'd been crying.

"I'm sorry. I fell asleep at Grand Nan's," Molly said lamely.

"What? She said you'd gone home."

"I know. I was out on the screened porch, and Grand Nan forgot I was there."

"Come *on*, Molly."

"It's true!" Molly cried. "You know she gets confused at night."

"Fine." Blair's anger was hard and flat, like a dull knife. "You can explain later." She kept a firm grip on Molly's arm as they climbed the hill, pushing her from behind as if she were a small child on the way to a spanking.

When they reached the house, they were both out of breath. The kitchen was overwhelming: a pungent odor of burning curry made Molly gag, and the bright light assaulted her swollen eyes. She wanted to run upstairs to the dark quiet of her bedroom, but she didn't dare. Instead, she watched helplessly while Blair rushed to the stove, turned off the gas, and thrust the smoking pot into the sink, drenching it with tap water. Steam billowed and hissed into Blair's face.

"Dinner's ruined!" Blair cried, throwing a wooden spoon angrily at the pot. Yellow stains splattered across the white porcelain. Blair whirled on Molly, her eyes blazing. "You can't do that!" she said fiercely. "Run off and not say where you're going—"

"I'm sorry!" Molly interrupted, her voice as shrill as Blair's. "I told you, I fell asleep. And I can go to Grand Nan's without telling you. I'm not a baby anymore!"

"Really? Sometimes I wonder," Blair snapped. "All you think about is yourself. There are other people in this house who have problems and worries of their own. You are *not* the center of the universe, Miss Molly. Even though Mark and Grand Nan give you a different message." She bit her lip, but it was too late to take the words back.

Molly backed toward the door. "Don't talk about my grandmother that way," she said slowly, leaving a careful space between each word. She couldn't cry now. "Or my father. I'm going back to Grand Nan's. She understands why I'm upset. You don't."

Blair flinched as though slapped, and grabbed Molly by the elbow. "How can I understand if I don't know what's wrong?" She took a deep breath. "I was worried sick. It made me furious." She grabbed a clean dish towel, ran it under hot water, and gave it to Molly. "Here. Wash your face. Then sit down. We'd better talk."

Molly sponged her face. "You wouldn't treat me like this if Dad were home," she whispered, feeling an angry satisfaction when pain flickered in Blair's eyes. Serves you right, Molly thought. She sank into the old armchair next to the woodstove, drew her legs up to her chest and hugged them, resting her cheek on the little table made by her knees. When Blair touched her arm, Molly jerked away, turning her head toward the stove. I won't talk to you, Molly thought. I won't. You can call me anything you like, but you're not my boss.

"Molly," Blair said, "please look at me. I apologize. Of course you may go to your grandmother's whenever you want. It's just common courtesy to tell people where you are, that's all."

I didn't want you to know, Molly thought, keeping her head down.

"I lost track of time in the darkroom," Blair admitted. "And then when I couldn't find you, I got scared. Were you sad about Mark leaving?"

Molly felt a little surge of power. Blair was that worried about her? She glanced up through her hair, which had fallen down across her cheek. "I wasn't upset about Dad," she said coldly, "it was something else."

"What?"

"I don't have to tell you."

"But you decided to confide in your grandmother." Blair stood in front of Molly, her arms folded across her chest.

"Yes," Molly said crossly. "Look, I'm sorry, OK? I've always told Grand Nan everything. She's the only one who will talk to me about my mother. She tells me stories about her. Sometimes—" Molly couldn't go on. She felt as if her face had crumpled around her mouth. She buried her head between her knees.

"Dear girl," Blair said softly. She rubbed Molly's shoulders. "So it's your mother again."

Molly felt hot tears soak through her blue jeans. She had to tell someone. But Blair? After the things she'd said?

"Sharing eases the pain sometimes," Blair said quietly.

Molly was silent for a long time, torn between anger and a slow, burning need to let the hurt out. At last, in half-clipped sentences that told only the bare minimum, Molly explained how she'd gone back to Sadie's a second time and found the old photographs. "Sadie decided to give me some clippings to read," Molly said. Her lip trembled. "They were pretty upsetting."

"What are they about?" Blair asked in a low voice.

"My mother's accident," Molly said dully.

"Sadie made you read about your mother's *death?*" Blair asked fiercely. "I could kick myself—I should never have pushed you to go there."

"It was my idea," Molly insisted. "Mine, and Grand Nan's."

"All right." Blair frowned. "But I don't understand. Why would she keep those articles? Why give them to you now?"

"I asked her about my mother." Now that she had started talking, Molly was tempted to tell Blair everything, to confess that she'd answered Ramon's letter and snooped around Sadie's house. But what if Blair told her father? Instead, Molly said, "Sadie decided I was old enough to know everything."

Blair was quiet a minute and then said, "If there's something hidden, I suppose it's time you heard about

it. But not from Sadie. From Mark, or your grandmother, perhaps."

When Molly still said nothing, Blair stood up. "You'd
better let me read the clippings," she said. "Where are
they?"

"I guess I left them in the shop." Molly's voice seemed
to come from some distant place outside her head. "I'll
get them." She tried to hoist herself out of the sunken
cushions but Blair pushed her down.

"Wait here. I'll be right back."

While she was gone, Molly's mind began to tingle,
like a hand that's fallen asleep and suddenly wakes up.
"Questions about Yuba River crash," a small jab said in
one part of her head. "Receiving my deed . . . Yuba
River," said another pinprick. "We lost her to that
geology," came Grand Nan's voice. "I'm writing about
your deceased wife, Ashley O'Connor . . ."

The pieces of the puzzle floated past and then something else jangled in her brain. The broken window!
Molly jumped up and hurried to the screen door as Blair
reappeared, running back from the barn with the manila
envelope flapping in her hand. Her face was grim in the
porch light.

"I'm sorry," Molly cried before Blair could speak, "it
was an accident."

"What happened?" Blair ran her eyes over Molly's
face, as if searching for clues to her strange new behavior.

"I was angry—I threw a block of wood at the wall, but
it missed."

To Molly's relief, Blair laughed. "It must have made a wonderful noise. Much more satisfying than tossing things in the sink. Never mind," she said, pushing Molly back inside, "we'll clean it up in the morning."

Molly joined Blair at the kitchen table and waited while she read through the clippings. Blair's brow was furrowed with concentration, as it was when she studied a print in the darkroom. She read everything, including the obituary, and whispered, "Poor Mark." Then she turned and brushed her fingertips lightly over Molly's hand. "I'm sorry you had to see this. What upset you the most?"

"Reading about her death like it was just a bunch of facts some reporter put down." Molly's voice shook precariously. "It made me see everything for the first time, as if I'd been there when it happened." She shut her eyes, trying to block the image of the truck hurtling out of control. "I don't understand," she said, twisting her hands in her lap. "What was my mother doing there anyway? And that man—it sounds like he was—" Molly bit her lip, trying to keep it from shaking.

"A boyfriend," Blair said quietly. She put her small hand over Molly's, squeezing gently. "It might have been innocent. After all, your father said she was doing research. Maybe he was helping her."

"Maybe," Molly said. "But then, why would Dad still be so angry? And why didn't he ever tell you about the accident?" Molly had always assumed her father told Blair everything, that the long, slow looks they shared were part of some secret code.

"I knew how she was killed," Blair said. Her eyes looked sad and tired. "But I never knew about the man—which makes sense, I suppose." She took a deep breath. "Molly, I don't know how to say this. When you're the second wife, and the first one has died, you feel as if you're on thin ice. You have to walk so carefully, to keep from falling through." Blair picked up a spoon and turned it over and over in her hands, smoothing the silver with her thumb. "You never think you can be good enough—as a wife, or a mother." She paused and glanced at Molly. "I don't know if I should say this or not."

"Go ahead," Molly said gruffly. Blair's trust made her feel ashamed of her own rude silences.

"I never wanted to ask about—Ashley," Blair went on, stumbling over Molly's mother's name as if she had never used it before. "I was afraid it would remind Mark of everything, remind you and Todd that I wasn't really your mother, when I wanted so much to be. I was afraid you'd compare me with her and feel sad for what you'd lost." Blair looked up again, and Molly couldn't remember when her eyes had ever seemed so soft.

"When you were interested in your mother, I have to admit it hurt," Blair said. "Even though I knew it was natural. In fact, I couldn't believe it took you this long to ask."

Just what Sadie said, too, Molly thought, but she didn't speak. She wanted Blair to keep talking.

Suddenly, Blair slapped the table with her open palm, startling Molly. "Blast that Sadie—she had no right to be so irresponsible." She looked at Molly carefully before asking, "What will you do now?"

Molly shook her head, pulling her father's shirt tight around her. She couldn't imagine moving beyond the throbbing hurt inside to continue her search. But she couldn't leave it unfinished either. If only she were five years old and someone would take her hand and tell her what to do!

As if she'd heard Molly's thoughts, Blair announced: "We're going out to dinner. Run upstairs and change." She strode to the sink, picked up the pot of lumpy curry, and dumped it into the garbage.

Molly gazed into Blair's small, heart-shaped face. She felt the same, deep tug inside that had jerked her at Sadie's, when she'd suddenly seen the dreary poverty of the old woman's life. Until this moment, she'd never considered what it must have been like for Blair to plunge into their family, how scary it must have been.

"I'm sorry you were worried," Molly muttered. "I should have told you where I was going."

"You were too upset," Blair said. "Forget about it. Now take off that dreadful shirt of Mark's and put on something bright. We're going out on the town."

Molly felt naked, like a crab that had sloughed off its hard, brittle shell, leaving softness exposed underneath. She took a deep breath, hugged Blair quickly and impulsively, and ran upstairs.

CHAPTER 12

Molly peeled off her clothes, jumped into the shower, and scrubbed her hair until it squeaked. She wrapped a towel around her head and rummaged in her closet for a shirt Blair had given her on her birthday in April. She'd never worn it—part of her stubborn resistance to anything that smelled suspiciously like "fashion." It was a soft cotton, blue and black flecked with streaks of silver. She let it hang loose over her clean blue jeans and stuck her feet into sandals rather than tennis shoes. At the last minute, she hooked a gold chain around her neck, something Grand Nan had given her a few years ago. "When she still remembered my birthday," Molly murmured.

She forced herself to look in the mirror as she combed the tangles from her hair. Her nose was still slightly swollen, but her eyes stared calmly back at her from the glass. Molly thought of the daguerreotype and the young woman's mischievous grin; she tried a quick smile now, in front of the glass.

Before she opened the door, she stared at her father's canvas shirt, lying in a heap on her hooked rug. Idiot, she thought. How could she wear this for hours, and never look for the letter? She searched the pockets, shoving her hands into each deep hole. They were all empty. A little start of fear tugged at her belly. Did her father have it with him? She shrugged. It was too late to worry, too late to stop things now. Molly felt as if she'd set her search at the top of a hill and given it a tiny push. It was rumbling down a mountain, gaining speed, an avalanche beyond her control.

Molly ran downstairs to find Blair waiting by the door. She had changed into a bright green Mexican top that matched her eyes, and her dark hair, freed from its clip, fell loosely over her shoulders.

"You look nice," Molly said.

"So do you." Blair sounded as shy as Molly felt. She scribbled a note to Todd on the blackboard by the phone and beckoned to Molly, as if they were embarking on a forbidden errand. "Forget the men. This is girls' night out."

Molly started to get in the car, then said, "Wait a minute." She ran to the barn and found the daguerreotype in the pocket of her windbreaker, which she'd left on the shop floor. She cradled it in her hands as they drove down the driveway.

They were both quiet while the tires hummed on the

dirt road. Molly leaned against the door, too drained to do more than breathe in the smells of the June night.

"What do you feel like eating?" Blair asked when they approached the outskirts of town. "Pizza? Fish? Something exotic?"

"Let's go to Angelo's," Molly said decisively. "I want a huge serving of lasagna."

Blair parked in front of the brightly lit windows of the Italian restaurant. They chose a booth in the back, set apart from the noise at the bar. Molly waved to a few friends from school and then ordered lasagna and a soda. Blair asked for linguine with clam sauce. When their drinks came, she took a slow sip of red wine and peered up at Molly from under her bangs.

"Cheers," she said, lifting her glass. "To summer."

Molly clicked her glass of ginger ale to Blair's and smiled, although she felt awkward.

"Remember the daguerreotype I showed you?" Molly asked later, when they'd eaten their salads.

Blair nodded. "Sure."

Molly pulled it from her pocket. "The newspaper article said my mom was found near the Yuba River." Molly spoke slowly, finding she could keep her voice steady as long as she avoided words like "killed" or "accident." "There's a connection between this picture and my mom," she continued, opening the clasp of the leather case. She unfolded the tiny piece of paper and let it rest gently in the palm of her hand like a moth, turning it sideways so Blair could read the slanted script.

"I don't understand," Blair said.

"This woman is receiving her deed at the Yuba River. Would that mean she's buying land?"

"Probably," Blair said. She looked at the picture. "She's digging, though." Her eyes were puzzled.

"Yuba River," Molly said, letting the words roll around in her mouth like something soft and juicy. "This woman was at the Yuba River. So was my mom. And," she added, deciding it wouldn't hurt to let Blair in on one more secret, "I looked it up in the atlas at home. Someone had underlined Yuba River on the road map. And in the index, too. I think it was Mommy."

Molly inhaled slowly. "Then—she died there, with some man."

Blair took a last bite of salad. "What are you thinking?"

Molly shrugged. "That she had some good reason for going to California. Something else, besides geology. But I'm not sure what. That's what I still need to figure out."

The waitress set a steaming casserole of lasagna in front of Molly, who inhaled the smell of garlic and tomato sauce. "I'm starving," she said. She took a bite of hot pasta, broke a piece of garlic bread from the loaf, and dipped it in the sauce. When the tastes had mingled in her mouth and warmed her stomach, she looked up. "Blair, please don't tell Dad if he calls. Not yet."

"All right." Blair twirled thin strands of linguine around her fork. "Aren't you angry at Sadie?"

"Sort of." Molly sipped her ginger ale and stirred the ice noisily with her straw. "But I asked her about Mommy, and it's worse when no one tells me anything."

Blair winced. "You mean the way Mark deals with it."

Molly nodded. "And you know what?" she added, surprising herself as she said it, "I think Sadie's lonely, but she's too proud to admit it."

Blair thought for a minute. "You may be right. But if she makes you break another window, we'll have to take a different approach."

Molly smiled. "OK." Now that her stomach was full, she was feeling different about everything. She propped the leather case open against the bread basket.

"Where is the Yuba River anyway?" Blair asked suddenly.

"Up in northern California. Why?"

"I just wondered. From the look on your face, I thought you might be on the next plane. Look, don't go *there* without giving me some warning."

"All right." Molly laughed. But something leaped inside her high as a colt jumping a fence. Go there, she thought. Of course. That's what she'd do. Go to the Yuba River, and see it for herself.

Molly slept late the next day and woke feeling hot and sweaty. Strong sunshine was pouring across the foot of her bed and the maple leaves whispered outside her window. She pulled on old shorts and a T-shirt and ran down to the kitchen, almost tripping over Crisco at the foot of the stairs. She scratched the dog behind the ears where her fur was thickly matted, then turned to the table. Propped against the cereal box were two letters addressed to Molly, and a note that said:

"Molly. Some mail for you—I didn't know you had friends in California! I loved our evening out. Blair."

Molly picked up the envelopes and studied the return address. "Ramon Rodriguez," she whispered. "Why did you write twice?" Molly opened the thick envelope first. It was sealed with Scotch tape. Inside were three letters: one from Ramon to Molly and two others, typewritten on thin onionskin, addressed to Miss Darby. Molly's hands shook as she read them, beginning with Ramon's:

Dear Molly O'Connor,

Thanks for your letter. I'm sorry about your mother. I didn't know she had kids. I guess you must have been little when she died.

Here are the letters she wrote Miss Darby. She told me to throw them away but I'm glad that I didn't.

It sounds as though your mother was looking for something important. Let me know if I can help. There isn't much to do here some days.

By the way, you asked about my job. It's OK, because I learn a lot about the people who first came out here in the Gold Rush. I guess Nevada City was crazy then. It's pretty dull right now. What's it like in Griswold, Vermont?

Gotta go
—from Ramon Rodriguez

Molly shook her head, then opened her mother's letter, taking a deep breath before she started to read.

Dear Miss Darby,

I'm doing some research on some of my ancestors and wonder if you might be able to help me. I'm looking for a woman named Abigail Parker who lived in your area around the time of the Gold Rush. Would the Historical Society have records about local residents of that period, or should I consult the town clerk? I need to know where she lived, when she was married, etc. Also, would any of her descendants still live in the area? I'm sure these questions may sound silly, but we've lost track of this branch of our family.

I'll be in Northern California next month, but decided to write ahead so you'd have time to look things up.

Molly's mother went on to say that she would call before she came to Nevada City. Molly shook her head. Nothing fit together yet.

The second letter was very short. Ashley wrote:

The letter you found is thrilling! I never dreamed you'd turn up something so interesting. Any chance there would be more from that correspondence? I look forward to meeting you next month.

Molly read everything twice, surprised that her mother's letters didn't touch her. It was hard to believe that the brisk, impersonal sentences were written by someone who would soon be hurtling toward her death in a stranger's truck.

"*You're* real, though," Molly sighed, touching Ramon's letter. "And alive." She spooned strawberries onto her cereal, wondering how old Ramon was. Molly took a bite of her breakfast and suddenly remembered the second envelope. She tore it open. Inside was a scrawled note from Ramon and two pages of faint photocopy.

> *Found this in Miss Darby's file after I mailed the letters. Sounds like your mother was onto something out here, doesn't it? Sorry this copy is so faint. There's no sign of the original— maybe your mother had it. Let me know if I should keep looking.*

Molly took the photocopied pages outside. The print was blurred and hard to read. She set them on the railing, in the sun, and saw that these were copies of old letters. Molly's heart began to race. Wasn't this the same, cramped script as the one inside her daguerreotype? She puzzled slowly over the words, wishing the copy were darker. The first page was dated *September 21, 1853,* and it read:

Dearest Caroline,

Last week on my eighteenth birthday I made claim to my own piece of land, five acres beside roaring Kanaka Creek, a tributary of the Yuba River. I paid for every inch of it with my own savings. I earned money by cooking for the miners, or bending over the "Long Tom" in the river, where we sift the gravel for gold. I've worked like a man, wearing Will's cast-off boots and trousers until Mother has given up on me.

The miners who eat their meals at Mother's "restaurant" (three long trestle tables set up under a tent) often pay us in gold dust. I collected my share in a tiny bag and slept with it under my straw tick for safety until I had more than enough gold coins, nuggets and currency to buy the land.

I'm sending you a likeness, taken to remember this day. The man in the picture is Mr. Eames of the Land Grant offices. My shovel marks the spot where I'll build a cabin next spring.

September 25

There's been so little time to write the last

few days. If my hand is hard to read, forgive me. I'm writing by candlelight.

Matthew's been so patient! I promised I'd marry when I had my own property. We'll be wed next time the minister comes through town. I'll hide my big gold nugget, the lucky chunk I found in the flood waters last spring, near the tiny apple tree I planted in May. The Kanaka Indians tell me a hidden stone brings good fortune and many children!

Dear Sister, how is your new baby? I pray you are happy and well.

Your loving sister,
Abigail Parker (soon to be Reed)

Molly clutched the letter and ran back inside. She did a little dance of excitement around the kitchen table, knocking over a chair. "The shovel marks the spot," Molly sang under her breath. She stood the chair back up and studied the pages again. Someone else had read this letter before. The paragraph about the gold nugget was circled with pencil and a scrawled note in the margin read: "Check Nevada City for deeds."

Molly scanned her mother's letter. There it was: Abigail Parker's name. "So that's who you are," she whispered. "Abigail Parker. Receiving your deed, somewhere near the Yuba River—on Kanaka Creek. It says so, right here."

Molly's heart was pounding. She felt as if she had a

jigsaw puzzle with all the pieces laid out in front of her, but no picture on the box lid to guide her. Her thoughts raced faster than her heart. Take it easy, she told herself.

She ran upstairs, grabbed the road atlas from her desk, and brought it outside. She found the California index again and noticed something she'd missed before. Yuba River wasn't the only place name that was under-lined. Higher up in the alphabetical list, someone had circled a town called Allegheny. Molly searched for Kanaka Creek, but didn't see it. Was it too small for a road map?

Molly crossed her arms and hugged herself. The atlas might have been shouting her mother's name. She ran her hand across the map, as if, ten years later, the page held the secret warmth of her mother's touch. She knew, Molly thought. She knew where the gold nugget was, and she went to find it. Now it's up to me to see if it's still there.

CHAPTER 13

Molly carried the letters upstairs, set them on her bed, and took out her mother's photograph. She remembered how her history teacher last year had brought in a picture of John Wilkes Booth. Ms. Parsons had divided his face down the middle with her hand. With one side covered, they saw a handsome actor, someone almost normal. But when the teacher switched sides, one leering eye revealed the insane man who had shot President Lincoln.

Molly tried this with her mother's photograph, covering half of her smiling face, then the other, looking for signs of a confusing, split personality. But her mother's smile was direct and symmetrical, and each eye held the same steady gaze. She looked innocent—and happy.

Molly gave up. She started to replace the folder under her pillow, then stopped. Why should she hide it?

Instead, she cleared a place on her dresser, using a dirty T-shirt to wipe the dust away, and opened the frame, placing it so she could see her mother's smile from every corner of the room.

She glanced at her bedside table. Where was the daguerreotype? "I must have left it downstairs," Molly said, and went outside to eat her breakfast. She stood on the front steps, tipping her face to the sun between bites. Then she left her empty bowl on the railing and went to the barn. First she searched the grass beneath the window, looking for shards of broken glass. Then she went inside to sweep up, grumbling to herself as she worked. Why did she have to break a window? That was stupid. She'd have to replace the glass, which would eat into her lawn-mowing money.

She unfolded a ruler, measured the window frame and scribbled the figures on a piece of scrap wood. Then she stapled a piece of plastic over the opening, picked up the box of pictures from Sadie's, and went back to the house, climbing the spiral staircase to the darkroom. Her shoes clanged noisily on the metal treads, but Blair didn't hear her. She was staring at something on her table while orchestra music soared on the radio.

"Blair!" Molly said.

Her stepmother looked up, startled, and smiled. "Morning, Mol." She leaned over to turn the music down while Molly studied the elaborate contraption on the counter. The shades were drawn, and two intense lights were aimed at the daguerreotype. The leather case seemed tiny on the table's white surface. Blair was adjusting the focus on a big camera, which sat on a tripod above the old photograph. "I borrowed the picture. I hope you don't mind—I thought I'd reshoot it and enlarge it. Is that OK?"

"Sure," Molly said, although it made her uneasy to have Blair think they were in this together. "You're taking a picture of a picture?" Molly asked.

"Yes. I don't know why I didn't think of it before. I hope this will work—it took me a few tries to get the angle right. And then there's the problem of the glass they printed it on—it's really a mirror. . . ." She climbed onto her chair, looked into the eyepiece of the camera, and then adjusted it again. "Just a few more shots, and I'll be done."

Molly waited while the shutter whirred twice. Blair stepped down from her chair, closed the leather case, and gave it back to Molly. "I'll be interested to see if it works—I've never done this before."

"Thanks," Molly said. "Say, Blair—is that how you do it with regular ones? "

"It's much easier. Why?"

Molly opened the box of old photographs. "Sadie tore these from Grand Nan's albums."

Blair frowned. "So your grandmother was right—she *was* stealing things. I wonder why?"

"She missed my mother. And you know what?" Molly admitted, "I was stealing, too. I took this box from Sadie's parlor, but she caught me."

Blair's eyes twinkled. "I'm beginning to see a new side

of Molly! And what will happen to the pictures now? Are you going to hide them here?"

Molly laughed, embarrassed. "No, Sadie said I could have them. And I thought maybe—if you had time to make copies—I could give them to Sadie and Todd."

She expected her stepmother to refuse, but instead Blair hugged her quickly. "I'd love to. You never ask me for anything, do you realize that? Pick the ones you want, and I'll reshoot them some evening. It won't take long." Her green eyes were lit with warmth. "I meant what I said, Molly—I loved our dinner together."

"Yeah, it was fun," Molly said. She felt awkward all of a sudden. She gave Blair a shy smile, and quickly left the room.

For the next hour, Molly sat closeted in her bedroom, surrounded by letters, maps, and pictures. When she heard Kai calling her name downstairs, she stuffed Ramon's letter into her back pocket and shouted, "I'm up here!" Kai pounded up the stairs and opened the door before Molly could clean up the rest of her things. She quickly swept them aside.

Kai stood on the threshold a minute, blinking, her narrow eyes sweeping the room. "So, are we speaking yet?" she asked.

Molly laughed, embarrassed. "Sure. Why not."

Kai dropped onto the rug by Molly's bed, spreading her legs in a wide V, her back straight as a dancer's. "Remember that time we didn't talk for weeks?"

Molly nodded. "What a dumb fight. You said those poisonous berries at Grand Nan's were edible—"

"I still think they are!" Kai interrupted.

Molly laughed. "Let's not start again."

"Good. I hate it when we argue. I start missing you."

Molly flinched and turned away. When she looked up again, her friend's dark eyes were dancing, holding back laughter.

"What's so funny?" Molly demanded.

"Have you forgotten that it's summer vacation? Looks like you're writing a report." Kai pointed to the pile of clippings and letters.

Molly hesitated. Last time she let Kai in on her private thoughts, she'd wound up with hurt feelings.

"I won't say anything," Kai said quickly, as if she'd read Molly's mind.

Molly closed her door, then squatted on the rug next to her friend. "This is really secret," she said. "Remember how we used to prick our fingers, share our blood, and promise not to tell? Well, this is more serious than that." She hooked her hair behind her ears. "You can't talk to anyone about it, even Todd."

Kai lowered her eyes, then ran her index finger over her lips to seal them. "OK, I promise—they're zipped shut."

Molly took a deep breath. "When I went back to Sadie's, she wasn't there. Remember how she pushed you, when you opened the bake oven door? Well, I looked inside and found a box full of pictures of my mother. Sadie stole them from Grand Nan's albums."

"Weird." Kai grinned. "So you grabbed it and got away?"

Molly was tempted to make her adventure seem more exciting, but she couldn't lie to her friend. "Afraid not. She caught me. But we talked—and then she gave me these clippings. Look." She showed Kai the newspaper stories.

Kai glanced at the headlines. "Do I have to read them? Just give me the bare facts."

Molly explained about the crash and the unknown man in the truck, surprised that she was able to talk about it without shaking.

"Who was the guy?" Kai asked softly.

"Just what I wanted to know. I was really upset."

"Yeah, I'll bet. It would make me feel awful, if I found out my parents were doing that stuff."

Kai's voice was unusually low and gentle, and Molly's heart warmed. For once her friend seemed genuinely focused and interested in her. "Then I got these letters from California," she continued, showing Kai the photocopies.

Her friend squinted and then complained. "Who can read *this* stuff?"

"It doesn't matter," Molly said eagerly. "I can explain. Abigail Parker, who wrote this letter, is the woman in the old picture I showed you." Molly rummaged through the piles on her bed until she found the leather case. She opened it and smiled at Abigail, wanting to speak to her, to tell her she was about to unlock her secret, but Kai's presence stopped her. Instead, she touched the glass gently and took a deep breath.

"You *swear* you won't tell?"

"I promise!" Kai held her hands open in front of Molly, jangling the bracelets she wore on each wrist. "Look, no crosses."

Molly laughed to think Kai would still use their old signal. "OK. Listen, Abigail Parker says in her letter that she would bury *gold* near her cabin under an apple tree."

"Really!" Kai's dark eyes flashed. "So you're hoping it's a treasure hunt, not a love story."

"Kai—just because *you'd* only go there for a guy!" Molly cried. She studied her friend. "Seriously, do you think that's why mommy went—to be with him?" When Kai shrugged, she gave her one of her mother's letters. "Here, read what she wrote to the woman in California."

"No thanks." Kai tossed the letter back quickly, as if it had burned her. "Sorry, but that's weird—touching something of your mother's. Doesn't it make you feel strange?"

"I don't think Mommy would mind," Molly said, surprising herself. Her stomach turned over. It's beginning to happen, she thought, with a little blur of excitement. My mother's turning into a real person.

Kai stood up. "Come on, time for the juicy part," she said, with her hands on her hips. "There's only one person who could have sent you those letters, right? What did he say?"

Without thinking, Molly clapped a hand over her pocket. "That's private."

"Hand it over," Kai said, lunging toward her. Molly twisted out of reach and backed up against the wall, her cheeks burning. Kai giggled. "Just tell me—does he sound cute!"

"How should I know?" Molly exploded, laughing. "He's got messy handwriting, like Todd. He's probably a nerd. What kind of kid wants to work for a historical society—a bookworm? Maybe I'll find out what he's like when I go there—" Molly caught her breath.

"WHAT!" Kai screamed. "You're going to—"

Molly clapped her hand over Kai's mouth, muffling her voice before she could say "California."

"Kai, you *promised* you wouldn't say anything," Molly pleaded. "Let's go outside and I'll explain." She gathered everything up, including the atlas, and stuffed it in her backpack. They went outside and ran down the driveway to the bridge. Kai's bike lay in the long grass, next to Molly's.

"You parked here?" Molly asked.

"I thought you might be on our rock. I looked for you there," Kai admitted. "It made me kind of sad. I sat on the bank and thought about all the games we used to play. Maybe we shouldn't grow up."

"I guess we don't have much choice, do we?" Molly said.

They smiled at each other and then Kai asked, "So when are you going to call Ramon?"

"*Call* him? Why should I do that?"

"How else are you going to find out where the gold is? You can't just show up in California and go wandering around, looking for an old apple tree."

Molly felt defeated. Of course, the whole idea was impossible. She couldn't afford it. Besides, her parents wouldn't let her fly out there alone.

Kai kicked a stone with the toe of her sneaker and watched it fall into the water. "I know—we'll go to my house. No one's home. You can call Ramon from there."

"What will your parents say when they get the phone bill?"

"No problem. We'll make something up."

Molly wasn't convinced, but twenty minutes later, she sat cross-legged on Kai's canopy bed with a pink phone in her lap. "How do I get the number?" she asked.

"Look." Kai opened the phone book to the map of the United States. "Here are the area codes—oh, no, California has a whole bunch. Where is this place?"

"Nevada City. Wait a minute." Molly opened her backpack and pulled out her atlas. "It's near Sacramento." Molly looked up at Kai, paralyzed. "What will I say?" she wailed.

"To the operator?"

"No—to Ramon," Molly said desperately. Kai never understood why these things were so hard for her.

"You'll think of something. Here, I'll get his number." Kai dialed Information, wrote the numbers down, and gave the phone back to Molly. "Now. Just tell him who you are and what information you need. Simple. Then ask him if he's cute."

"Kai!" Molly squealed. "I don't call boys. I never do."

"So maybe he's grown up. In college or something."

"That would be even worse." But Molly took a deep breath, picked up the receiver, and dialed. To her dismay, a male voice answered on the first ring.

"Nevada City Historical Society."

"Ah, hello," Molly gasped. "Is Ramon there? Ramon Rodriguez?"

"Speaking."

Molly stared at Kai, panic-stricken. *Now* what?

"Hello?" Ramon said.

"Say something, you goof," Kai hissed, pinching Molly's ankle.

"Ouch—sorry." Molly nearly hung up, she was so embarrassed. "This is Molly O'Connor, from Vermont—"

"Oh, right!" Ramon's voice sounded younger as he interrupted her, and Molly nearly laughed with relief. "Boy, am I glad you called," he went on easily, chatting as if they were old friends. "I was kinda confused. I got a letter from your father today—but I thought he told you to write me?"

"Well, not exactly," Molly stammered, and then decided it was best to tell the truth. "Actually, he doesn't know about my letters," she blurted, hoping Ramon wouldn't hate her.

Ramon laughed. "Hey, I don't blame you. Parents can be weird. If I'd known you'd existed, I would have written you first."

"Really? Thanks." Molly felt warm inside; she shifted the phone to her other hand and wiped her sweaty palm on her shorts.

"Parents have a way of screwing things up," Ramon continued. "Like your dad, for instance. Don't get me wrong, he's probably nice and all, but he told me to destroy the letters."

"He did?" Molly thought about this a minute, then decided it made sense. Maybe her father was afraid the letters had to do with the boyfriend—if that's what he was. "I guess that's good, isn't it?" she said out loud. "I mean, he won't have to know I have them."

Molly settled back against the pillows, surprised by how relaxed she felt. The phone made her feel safe; she didn't have to worry about how she looked or where to put her hands, all the things that usually bothered her when she was face-to-face with a boy. Kai was stretched out on her side, propped up on her elbow, straining to hear Ramon's voice.

"Those old letters explained a lot," Molly said, and she told Ramon what she was guessing about her mother's interest in the buried gold. She omitted only the painful part of the story: the stranger with the pickup truck. When she finished, Ramon whistled.

"Have you considered a career in police work?" he asked.

Kai clapped a hand over her mouth to stifle a giggle; Molly nudged her with one foot and inched farther away on the bed.

"Not really," she said.

"Listen," Ramon said, "this is exciting. Do you think you had an ancestor in the Gold Rush? Everyone out here pretends they do, but most people are like my family—we showed up when it was over. Did this woman come all the way from Vermont to California?"

"I don't know." Molly realized she hadn't even thought about that part of the mystery. She'd studied "Westward Expansion" in school, but somehow the people in covered wagons seemed as flat and remote as the pages in her history book.

"Well, you've come to the right person," Ramon said. "Panning's my hobby. I do it with friends almost every weekend. Too bad you don't live around here, I could show you how."

Kai nudged Molly's foot and raised her eyebrows. Molly ignored her. "Do you ever find anything?" she asked.

"Not much. A little gold dust now and then. Nothing like this Abigail Parker, whoever she was. But listen, this call will cost a fortune. What should I do next?"

"Is there some way to find out where Abigail Parker had her homestead?" Molly asked. "She says she had five acres on Kanaka Creek."

"Maybe. There are some old land records here. People always come in asking about that stuff—and sometimes we have to call the County Office. Want me to do that for you?"

"That would be great. You don't mind?"

"Are you kidding? That's much more interesting than dusting old Darby's desk. What else?"

Molly hesitated. "Listen—this may sound funny," she blurted, "but you won't go looking for the gold, will you?"

Ramon didn't answer at first. "Think I'd steal from you?" he said finally. "Forget it. I'm not that type. In fact, I'll send you my picture so you can see how honest I look, and you send me one of yourself. Is that a deal?"

"Sure." Molly cleared her throat. Her voice had suddenly gone husky.

"Listen, what's your phone number?" Ramon added. "It might be easier for me to call you, when Darby's not here."

Molly gave him her number at home and said good-bye. She sprawled across the bed, her arms thrown out to the sides. Kai's canopy threw lacy shadows on the ceiling overhead. "Wow," Molly sighed, "he sounds wonderful."

Kai laughed. "Looks like you're in love."

"It's true," Molly said. "I am—in love with a voice on the phone."

CHAPTER 14

For the next hour Molly walked slowly, as if moving through water. Her arms and legs carefully parted the moist summer air as she and Kai made cheese sandwiches and carried them outside to sit under the wide canopy of the sugar maples. When Molly sat holding her sandwich, forgetting to take a bite, Kai cupped her hand over her mouth like a megaphone and said in a rasping voice, "Earth to Molly, Earth to Molly, do you read me?"

Molly smiled and tried to pay attention while Kai told her that the final tryouts for *Midsummer Night's Dream* were the next morning at the Playhouse. The director had asked Kai if she'd like to audition for the role of a fairy. "It's a real part with lines," Kai said, and disappeared to find her copy of the play.

Molly rolled onto her back and tried to match her

137

breathing to the slow rise and fall of the leaves above her. *Midsummer Night's Dream,* Molly thought idly. I'm in a midsummer *day's* dream. She closed her eyes and tried to imagine Ramon's face, replacing her first impression (a bookworm with thick glasses) with an image that matched his warm, teasing voice. She hardly noticed when Kai returned and sat beside her. Molly let Kai's murmuring of lines become a droning harmony beneath the remembered snatches of Ramon's conversation. When Kai suddenly hurled her book against the tree and curled up in a ball, clutching her knees, Molly leaped to her feet, astonished.

"Kai—what's *wrong?*"

"I'll never be able to do this. Never, never, *never,*" Kai said, thumping the ground with her fist.

Molly stared. "Why not?"

"I've been trying and trying to learn the lines, and I can't remember a single one."

"How many are there?"

"Only ten."

Molly crouched next to her friend, trying to see into her face. "I don't get it—how did you learn the lines for your school play?"

"I didn't." Kai tore at the grass, pulling it out in clumps and scattering them across her legs.

"What do you mean?" Molly asked.

Kai kept her head turned away so that Molly had to lean forward to hear her. "I didn't have any lines. My part was all pantomime. I never spoke." Finally she looked up. Tears spilled down her face. "No one knows except my mom and dad. I *can't* memorize. The acting teacher thought I was a genius. Ha. When he learns the truth, that's the end of my acting career."

Kai began to sob so hard she couldn't speak. She jumped to her feet and ran, stumbling around the corner of the house to the backyard, her sandals slipping awkwardly from side to side. Molly followed her soundlessly and watched as Kai dropped onto the old swing that dangled from the thick branch of a pine tree. Kai stabbed the ground angrily with her feet; her head snapped back and forth and the swing sailed into a curving arc.

Molly stood still for a moment, her elbows pinned tightly to her sides. Then suddenly she was moving before she had planned to. She snatched at the chain on the swing, ran with it, and dragged it to a stop. Kai tumbled forward onto the grass and collapsed in a heap, still crying.

"It's OK, Kai," Molly said, patting her friend's shoulder in a light rhythmical movement. "Please don't cry. I'll help you."

"How?" Kai's voice was muffled and sodden with tears. She wiped her nose with the back of her hand and turned her wet face to Molly. "It's easy for you to say." Kai rubbed her hands up and down her bare arms. "You don't know what it's like. You're smart. School's easy for you. I'm dumb, don't you know that? Dumb, dumb, dumb. Sure, I can act, but what good is it, if I can't remember the lines? I'll never be an actress. Never. It's just a stupid dream." Her eyes blazed as the tears poured down, unchecked.

"You're so lucky," Kai gulped. "Sometimes, in the last few years, I've almost hated you. I'd see your report card and think, why can't I do that? I don't *feel* dumb inside. But my brain doesn't work—didn't you see how I avoided reading the newspaper stories? I'm embarrassed for you to see how long it takes me."

Molly was shocked. She looked at her friend as though she'd become a complete stranger. In all the years they'd played together, Kai rarely mentioned school. Molly knew, from low conversations she'd overheard among their parents, that Kai worked with tutors and struggled to keep up. But her friend had such a careless way of talking about schoolwork, tossing it away like an old gum wrapper, that Molly thought she didn't mind doing badly. She just assumed that other things were more important to Kai. Things like sitting at a crowded table in a coffee shop, talking in different voices until her friends were doubled up with laughter. Or having two boys call and ask her to the same party. Or wandering through a shopping mall, snatching an outrageous sequined shirt off the rack, and buying it on the spot. These were vivid memories Molly had stored away after visits to the Stewarts' home outside Boston. She knew it took Kai all summer to read one or two books, while Molly could finish a thick one in a few days. But so what?

"Forget it!" Molly said, finding her voice at last.

Kai looked up, surprised, and said, "Forget the play? Yeah, maybe you're right."

Molly sat down beside her in the grass. "I mean forget it, because you're not dumb," Molly said. "So you have trouble learning. There's a kid like that in my class. He has a learning disability or something, but he's smarter than I am. So are you. So what if I read fast? I'm a klutz with people." Her own voice trembled now, but she pushed on, hurtling through the words as if she might never be able to say them again. "You're my only real friend. Everyone likes you. Not just Todd," she added, and Kai grinned a little.

"My dad says you've got street smarts," Molly continued. "He says you're the only kid he knows who could compete with him in a storytelling contest."

"He does?" Kai's face shone and she bit her lip. "Your dad tells great stories."

"Yeah, if you haven't heard them a hundred times," Molly said dryly. "Listen, Kai, I *know* you'll be an actress someday."

Kai's chest stopped heaving, and she glanced at Molly. "Do you really think so?"

"Of course. Think of all the plays we put on down by the brook."

"You made them up," Kai said quickly.

"Sometimes," Molly admitted, thinking how her imagination could leap forward, spilling ideas like a bowl of popcorn overturned on a rug. "But you know how to act them out. You were like the director. You made things seem real so I could follow you."

Kai looked at Molly. Her eyes were still wet, and thin streaks of black eye makeup smudged her high cheekbones. "Thanks," she said softly.

"Maybe you'll be a mime," Molly went on, excited now. "Like Marcel Marceau. Come on." She yanked at Kai's arm, pulling her up.

"Where are we going?"

"To get that book. I'm going to help you learn your lines."

Kai stood up numbly and followed Molly. "What's that dumb song on the radio?" Kai asked suddenly. "As long as we're together nothing can go wrong——" She looped her arm through Molly's and hugged her sideways. "'We're still together." She let go quickly, embarrassed, and Molly felt her own face burn.

"I have lots of other friends, but I could never say this to them," Kai said. "At home, I have to be cool. Nothing's supposed to phase old Kai. Hey—what's the matter?"

Molly stood frozen, laughing. "Singing—that's it!" she said.

"Huh?"

"Listen, Kai, you remember the words to all the songs on the radio, right?"

"Yeah—so what?"

"So Shakespeare's like singing. The lines are bouncy— our English teacher showed us when we read *Macbeth*. You know that part: 'Double, double toil and trouble—' "

" 'Fire burn and cauldron bubble,' " Kai finished. "*Everyone* knows that."

"But lots of Shakespeare is that way," Molly said. "We'll put it to music. It will work. I promise."

Kai flushed. "You really think so?"

Molly nodded. As they walked back to the front yard, she cleared her throat. "You know what's dumb? I thought you didn't like me because I was so immature."

Kai shook her head. "Uh-uh. I was jealous. Here I was, all excited about acting, but I was faking it. Underneath I was really scared. And then I found out you had this thing that was so real, almost like a quest in King Arthur—searching for your mother. It made me feel like—I don't know, like a nobody."

Molly's insides quivered. She'd always been afraid to let Kai—or anyone—get this close. But it's not so bad, she thought. I've told her everything I was feeling and nothing horrible has happened yet. "I thought I was the nobody," Molly said, "because I didn't have a mother."

"Now that really *is* dumb," Kai laughed. "Maybe two nobodies make a somebody," she added. "Double double—we might be double trouble, together. Wait until we find a way to fly you to California."

"*And* get you in the play," Molly said. "Come on, let's go learn your part."

CHAPTER 15

Molly rehearsed with Kai for the rest of that day and again the next afternoon when they biked slowly to the theater, throwing the lines back and forth to each other across the dirt road. Leaving Kai at the Playhouse entrance, Molly said, "If you forget your lines, just fake it and act. That's what they care about."

Kai licked her lips nervously, then straightened up, tossing her head until her long earrings glittered. She put her hand on the door. "Wish me luck," she whispered and slipped inside without looking back.

Biking home, Molly's skull hummed with the tune she and Kai had set to the fairy's words. " *'You spotted snakes with double tongue, Thorny hedge-hogs be not seen,'* " Molly chanted, throwing open the door and pointing at Todd. He sat at the kitchen table eating cereal, his bare, freckled legs stretched out in front of him.

"What are *you* so excited about?" he demanded, wiping milk from his upper lip.

" '*Newts, and blind-worms, do no wrong; Come not near our Fairy Queen,*' " Molly intoned, spinning across the kitchen with her arms spread wide. When the phone rang, Todd lunged for it from his seat as Molly tried to scoop it up. They scuffled at the edge of the counter. The receiver fell to the floor and dangled helplessly until Todd grabbed it and choked "Hello?" He held Molly at arm's length with one hand keeping her waving arms from the phone, listened a minute, then grinned. "Sure, she's here. Are you sure you want to speak to her? I think she's gone nuts."

"Todd!" Molly snatched the phone from her brother. " '*You spotted snake with double tongue,*' " Molly said into the receiver. "Did you get the part?" She waited for Kai to say something, and then, when there was silence, added, "You didn't forget your lines, did you?"

"I'm not sure I ever knew them," said a deep voice.

Ramon. Molly almost dropped the phone. She doubled over the counter, hating Todd for spoiling everything, hating herself for behaving like an idiot.

"Hello," she stammered, careful not to say Ramon's name while Todd was listening. "I'm sorry—I thought you were my friend—"

"Sorry to disappoint you."

"You didn't. I mean—" Molly's face burned as she

struggled to explain. "I thought you were my friend Kai. I was helping her learn some lines from Shakespeare."

"Well, when you get my picture, you can decide if I'm a spotted snake or not."

Molly started to laugh and then froze when she noticed Todd. He was leaning against the refrigerator, drinking milk from the carton, and listening. "Can you hold on a minute?" Molly said to Ramon, then covered the mouthpiece with her palm. "This is private," Molly hissed at her brother. "Go away."

Todd nodded. "Sure. After I get my snack." He opened the bread box slowly, as if his wide hands were weighted, pulled out a loaf of bread, and began to search the dish rack for the bread knife.

Molly felt desperate. "Sorry," she said to Ramon, "my dumb brother—"

"Stop saying 'sorry.' I know what it's like. Pity me, I have three sisters, and one answers the phone in a Donald Duck voice. Like this: '*Hullo, hullo. May I help you?*'"

His squawking made Molly laugh. She couldn't help liking him. Maybe he was weird in real life, but he was great on the phone.

"Listen," Ramon said, "we'd better be quick. Miss Darby doesn't know she's paying for this call. I've found something—but what about your brother? Does he know about any of this?"

Molly glanced at Todd, who was staring at the toaster, waiting for the bread to pop. "Ah—no. Not really."

"OK. I'll be careful. Yesterday I poked around in Miss

Darby's files and found some clippings from the newspaper—"

He hesitated, but Molly reassured him. "I've seen those. Hold on." She covered the phone again and glared at Todd. "*Get out.* Do you have to spoil everything?" She punched the toaster, grabbed the hot bread, and tossed it at her brother. He caught it against his chest and stalked outside, carrying a jar of peanut butter and a knife.

"Whew," Molly said when the door slammed. "Now I can talk." She kept her voice low. "Ramon, can you hear me?"

"Sure. Hey, Molly, I'm sorry to bring this up. I mean, it's pretty terrible. This guy with the truck, Paul Leone—"

"I know. It's weird, isn't it?" Molly's thoughts began to spin, like stones tumbling in a rock polisher. "But I've been thinking—maybe he went to help my mother find the gold."

"Is that a guess?"

"Of course," Molly admitted. "My mother was interested in geology, not just gold. Maybe this guy was a geologist, too, or maybe he knew about mining. Could you find out?"

Ramon paused, then said, "Well, I suppose. But what if I find something that's—"

"It's all right," Molly said, knowing what he meant. "I need to know everything." And suddenly she knew this was true. The woman in the truck with Paul Leone was as much her mother as the woman who picked up stones on the highway or played with her daughter in the river. Someone has to patch all these women together, Molly decided.

Todd passed in front of the screen door, scowled at her, then disappeared. "Listen," Molly whispered, "I'm coming out there."

"To California? How? When?"

"I don't know," Molly said, wiping her free hand on her shorts. "I haven't figured that out. Somehow."

Ramon cleared his throat. "Can I ask you something— personal?" he said, sounding awkward.

"Sure." Molly was glad he couldn't see how hot her face was.

"This man, Leone—did your father know about him?"

"I'm not sure. Dad won't talk about any of it."

"That must be awful."

"Sometimes. Actually, I'm getting used to it." Ramon's kindness made Molly feel light. She gripped the phone to keep herself from floating up the stairs and out the roof toward Soldiers' Hill. "Listen, Ramon—can you find out any more about the accident?"

"Maybe. The guy who wrote this story still lives in town. He—" Ramon stopped talking. Molly heard a woman's voice in the background, and then Ramon said, sounding very formal and official all of a sudden, "Fine, Miss O'Connor. I'll get back to you as soon as I can. Good-bye."

Molly giggled. "Thanks so much, *Mister* Rodriguez."

She hung up and hugged herself hard, gripping her arms and squeezing her eyes shut. Then she slipped outside onto the porch, checking carefully to see if Todd was around. The yard was empty and the sun drew long shadows across the pasture as Molly dashed down the hill.

I'm finding her, river. The words slithered into her head as she hurtled along the path. She scrambled down the bank and had her shoes off before she saw Todd, sitting cross-legged on her rock.

"Beat you," he taunted.

Molly stared. "You can't sit there," she blurted.

"Why, you own the river or something?"

Yes, it's mine! Molly wanted to cry, but she realized how foolish it would sound. Instead, she bent to put her shoes back on.

"Hey, where you going?"

"Somewhere private where I can think in peace," Molly retorted, starting up the bank.

"Oh, no you don't." Todd splashed to shore in his sneakers and grabbed Molly's arm.

"Let me go!" Molly winced and pulled away.

Todd stood so close she could feel his breath. His red-brown eyes snapped with anger. "Who was that creep on the phone?"

"None of your business. *You're* the creep. I never talk to your friends about you that way." Molly's lip trembled.

"*So sorry*—I didn't know you had a new boyfriend."

"He's not my boyfriend! I hardly know him!" Molly clenched her fists and shook with the effort not to cry.

"Then why did you tell him about Mommy?"

"I didn't!" Molly cried, stunned.

"Don't lie. I heard you. 'My mother was interested in geology,' " Todd mimicked. " 'Can you find out anymore about the accident?' Man!" He paced up and down on the narrow bank, kicking at the stones with the toe of his sneaker. "So you like sharing family secrets?"

"Jerk!" Molly cried. "You spied on me. You never leave me alone. I hate you!" She whirled and started up the bank, but Todd yanked on the tail of her T-shirt and pulled her back. Molly stumbled to her knees, scrambled to her feet, and socked her brother hard, in the stomach.

"Hey!" Todd staggered backward, astonished. His face was the color of his hair: a deep, rusty red.

"If you tell anyone about that call, I'll never forgive you," Molly screamed. "Never, never, never." Hardly aware of how hard she was crying, Molly struck out again, but Todd jumped to the side, avoiding her.

"What do you think you're doing?" he said. "Talking about our mom's death to some total stranger?" Todd stood with his legs braced and his hands poised in front of him, ready for her next attack. "I guess you forgot she's my mother too," he said.

The shaking in his voice shut off Molly's tears. She was speechless for a moment and then said softly, "I didn't forget. It's just—" She hesitated. "I've found out some things about her, and I don't know if they're true or not. I didn't want to tell you until I was sure—"

"Oh, I see," Todd interrupted, his voice caustic, "we didn't suffer enough the first time, so you want us to be sad all over again. Give me a break. Don't dredge this up. And you might think about Blair, for once."

"She knows what I'm doing."

Todd stared. "She does?"

"She's helping me."

Todd scrubbed his hair with both hands and shook his head. "I don't get it." His eyes looked lost, like a little boy's. He turned away and spoke softly. "I was so frustrated last week, when you asked me about her. I couldn't remember *anything*. My mind was blank. As if someone had washed her away."

"That happens to me, too," Molly whispered. "Listen, I'm sorry. I'll tell you everything."

"I don't know if I want to hear it," Todd said.

But he stood there, waiting. In a low, halting voice, speaking to his wide back, Molly quickly told him about Ramon's letter, her trips to Sadie's, her hunch about the gold on Abigail Parker's land. Then she came to the hard part.

"She died in a pickup truck," Molly said softly, "with a man named Paul Leone. The reporter made it sound as if—he might have been a boyfriend, or something."

Todd was completely silent. His arms dangled at his sides, then his shoulders began to shake. Molly swallowed her fear and stepped forward to touch his arm. "I miss her too," she whispered. "It stinks."

To Molly's surprise, Todd whirled and staggered toward her, throwing his thick arms around her shoulders. Molly held her breath and stood rigid a moment.

Todd's wrenching cries came from some unused, rusty place deep in his stomach. Molly softened under his grip; she let her own arms encircle him, gingerly at first, then tightly as she felt his tears wet her hair. They stood there a long time before Todd finally pulled away.

He groaned, then crouched beside the river and splashed his face with water. "I haven't cried like that since she died." He cleared his throat. "If the papers made it sound like she was having an affair, and Dad won't talk about it—that makes it even worse. He must think she was crazy about the guy. Otherwise, he'd be more open about her, right?" When Molly didn't answer, he demanded, "Even if she *was* looking for gold, she still died in some stranger's truck. Who was he, anyway?"

"I don't know yet. Maybe he was a boyfriend. Or maybe—he was helping her." Molly knew this was wishful thinking, but she didn't care. "Does it matter?"

"Of course it does," Todd said. "Either she was behaving like an idiot, hurting Dad—or she was doing something legitimate, and died because the guy drove like a maniac." He pressed his thumbs against his temples. "Thanks for the massive headache," he said. "What am I supposed to do now?"

"Scream and throw things," Molly said with a grim smile. "That's what I did."

"Really?" Todd raised an eyebrow. "My sweet sister?" As he spoke, he bent over, grabbed a stone, and hurled it across the river. Molly felt his anger in the sharp flick of his wrist. The rock ricocheted off a tree on the opposite bank, and soon the river resounded with the sound of stones hitting boulders, thunking against trees. With every toss, Todd grunted and swore, then he howled, a sound that made Molly shiver.

Molly backed away from the riverbank, afraid to stay, afraid to leave. She closed her eyes and covered her ears, but nothing could shut out the sight of her brother, his feet braced in the current, his head thrown back to the sky. And nothing, not even the river's song, could drown his angry cursing, which bounced off the wooden timbers of the bridge and brought silent tears to Molly's eyes.

CHAPTER 16

Molly stood at the kitchen sink the next morning, letting warm water run across her wrists while she thought about Todd. After the water fight, his face had been smooth but drained as they sat by the river and watched the wind toss the trees. Later, they climbed the hill, wet and shivering, and huddled in Molly's room where she showed him the clippings, Abigail's letter, and their mother's correspondence with Miss Darby. When she was done, Todd grew silent. At dinner, he picked at his food and excused himself before dessert. When Molly found him later, he was sound asleep on his bed, still dressed, his arms flung out to the sides and a baseball cap drawn over his face. Molly had tiptoed through the litter of dirty clothes and car magazines to turn off his light, feeling more like a mother than his kid sister.

Now, squirting soap over last night's dishes, Molly

wondered if she'd told Todd too much. Of course, she'd been vague about Ramon. She didn't trust her brother not 'to tease her, and she wanted to keep Ramon to herself. Ramon's conversation still buzzed inside her head. Molly tried to remember the way he laughed, the soft tone when he said: "That must be awful."

She looked out the window. A heavy mist had settled on the river, and the trees shimmered like wet ghosts. Molly almost expected them to move, 'and was startled when a figure burst from the fog on the brow of the hill and came running toward the house.

"Kai," Molly said. She turned off the water and ran out on the porch, wiping the soapsuds on her jeans. "You got the part?" Molly called when she saw Kai's face.

Kai ran up the steps, out of breath, and stood in front of Molly, grinning. "How did you know?"

"The way you look. Congratulations!" Molly fingered Kai's blouse, a dazzling blue studded with rhinestones and enormous batik circles. "New shirt?" she asked.

Kai shook her head. "It belongs to Maya. The woman at the theater. We traded clothes."

"The actress with the braid," Molly said. Was it just last week she was so jealous of Kai and Maya whispering backstage? Everything had happened so quickly.

"She's nice," Kai was saying. "She's older—in college, but she might drop out." She tossed her hair and smiled. "Know what? I did forget a line, but I faked it, just like you said. The director liked that the best. She said it was good I could improvise."

"So when do rehearsals start?"

"Tomorrow. You can come if you like."

"Maybe." Things changed so fast from day to day, Molly couldn't predict tomorrow anymore, or even the next few hours. "I have to finish the dishes—want to come in?"

"Sure." Kai followed Molly inside and perched on the counter, swinging her long legs in their skintight jeans. Molly rinsed the plates and stacked them in the rack while Kai, laughing, told her about the director's fight with one of the actors, how she'd thrown a chair at him across the stage. "Boy, everyone was freaked," Kai said. "I hope she never does that to me."

As they laughed, the door to the back stairs flew open and Todd stumbled in, his face creased with sleep.

"Hey, Todd," Molly said. She felt suddenly shy, as if they hardly knew each other. She wondered what Kai would have said if she'd heard the wracking sound of his sobbing or his voice accusing Molly: "*She's my mother too.*"

"You don't work today?" Kai asked.

Todd shook his head. "Think I'll call in sick."

Kai laughed. "*Are* you?"

"Sure. Sick of work." He disappeared into the pantry and came out mumbling, "There's nothing to eat. Doesn't anyone go to the store around here?"

Molly realized she'd hardly seen Blair the last few days. "Blair's living in the darkroom again."

Todd laughed. "Yeah. She forgets to come out." He found a stale bagel in the bread box and tore bites from it while he asked casually, "Hey, Mol, is Kai in on this stuff?"

"About Mommy?" She took a deep breath. "Yeah."

Molly expected him to be angry, but instead, he smiled. "Good. We don't have to pussyfoot around—at least, not until Friday."

"What happens then?" Molly demanded.

"Dad comes home."

Molly wet her lips with her tongue. Would she have to tell Dad what she'd been doing?

"How about going over to Sadie's this morning?" Todd asked.

Molly stared. "All of us? Why?"

"Since she gave you those articles, I wondered if she's hiding something else—about our mother."

"Maybe," Molly said. She thought of Sadie's drawers, full of baby shoes, the oven with its acrid smell. "But I don't think—"

Before she could finish her sentence, they heard steps on the porch and Blair sidled in, hung with cameras in plastic pouches. An old, battered hat covered her hair. "Great morning for pictures," she said, smiling.

"Really?" Todd said. "Doesn't look so good to me."

"The light is perfect." She stared at Todd as if noticing him for the first time. "Todd. What are *you* doing home?"

"Playing hooky."

"I don't know if I like that."

Todd shrugged. "I haven't missed a day yet."

"All right. But you'd better give the lumberyard a call." Blair looked at the three of them and set her cameras on the table. "So, why the guilty looks. What's up?"

"We were just talking about going to Sadie's," Todd said.

Blair glanced at Molly. "All of you?"

Molly nodded. "Todd knows," she said.

"I'm glad." When no one said anything else, Blair beckoned to Molly. "Can you come upstairs a minute?"

Molly followed her stepmother into her studio where Blair picked up the heavy dictionary on her table and drew out a stack of pictures. "These are nice and flat now," she said, and handed the top one to Molly. "A present."

Abigail Parker looked up at Molly from the print, her smile still cocky, although the enlargement made her face seem grainy and pale. "Thanks," Molly said.

"Look closely," Blair said, pointing to a corner of the print where the trunk of a pine tree protruded into the frame.

Molly squinted. The enlargement was blurred, but she could make out a crude sign nailed to the tree: a slanted board painted with crooked letters. "What does it say?" Molly said. "K-E—" She looked at Blair.

"I couldn't read it either, but I thought it was just my old eyes. Here, try this." She handed Molly a magnifying glass.

Molly held the glass over the photograph. "Kenton—Mine?"

Blair nodded. "That's what it looked like to me. Does that mean anything to you?"

"Probably some old gold mine—it must be gone by now." Molly sighed. "When was the Gold Rush, anyway?"

"Eighteen forty-nine." Blair smiled. "Maybe your secret source in California could find out if the mine still exists."

Molly shot Blair a suspicious look. "What'd you do—read my mail?" she demanded.

"Of course not, hon," Blair sighed. "But I did see the California postmarks, remember? I don't mean to pry," she added, "but I wanted to ask you—did the letters tell you anything else about your mother?"

You *are* prying, Molly thought, even though she knew Blair just wanted to help. "They were about Mommy's trip," Molly answered carefully. "And why she went. I can't explain it yet."

"Fair enough," Blair said, but her voice was small and quiet.

Molly studied the enlargement again. Even blown up, Abigail's smile was full of mischief. Molly wondered if her mother had ever seen the daguerreotype. If only her mother were still alive! Molly glanced guiltily at Blair, but her stepmother was turning off the lights, closing the darkroom door.

"Mrs. Stone's away today, so I'm going to check on your grandmother. I'll give you a ride to Sadie's, if you want."

They went downstairs. As they passed through the

unfinished room, kicking aside long curls of wood shavings, Molly caught her stepmother's arm. "Blair, I have to talk to Dad myself. Before you say anything to him."

"Of course." Blair turned to give her a hug, but Molly twisted away, ignoring the sudden hurt that sprang into her stepmother's eyes.

By the time they reached Sadie's, a fine mist was falling. "It always rains when I come here," Molly complained. She was on the porch before Blair had even turned the car around, with Todd and Kai following close behind her. She pounded on the door, but there was no answer. "The Chevy's here," Molly said nervously.

Todd went to the end of the porch and peered around the corner. "The yard's empty," he said. "Looks like a haunted house."

Molly took a deep breath. "It always does. Let's go in." Todd and Kai followed her through the kitchen and into the parlor. Two wooden racks full of clothes gave the room a wet, steamy smell. "Sadie?" Molly called. No one answered. Rain hissed gently into the gutters.

"What are we looking for?" Kai asked.

"I don't know." Molly looked at her brother. "This was your idea."

"I know." Todd threw Kai a knowing smile that made Molly's heart sink. "My sister's got this weird idea that our mother was on a treasure hunt," Todd told Kai, as if Molly weren't standing right beside him. "If you read the newspaper stories, it's pretty obvious Ashley had something else in mind—like a man." His voice was bitter and Molly wished she'd never told him anything.

"Maybe Ashley was looking for gold," he continued. "At least I thought so last night. But this morning I woke up and thought: Wait a minute. Do you really think she was crazy enough to travel all the way across the country just because some woman buried gold under a tree more than a hundred years ago? Or was she just running after a guy, to hurt Dad—" He smashed his fist into his open palm.

"Couldn't you both be right?" Kai pleaded.

"*Ashley*," Molly accused her brother. "So, she's 'Ashley' to you. Well, I still call her 'Mommy.' What makes you think she *wasn't* looking for gold?"

"Everything," Todd said carefully. "It doesn't hang together. But that's why we're here, to find out." He glanced out the windows, then opened the drawer in a small end table. It was empty. "Where did Sadie hide everything?"

"I don't have to tell you," Molly said in a low voice. "You can trash Sadie's house if you want. I've got my own way of finding things." She whirled and started toward the kitchen. Tears blurred her eyes so she didn't see Sadie. She ran straight into her, nearly falling over backward as the old woman strode into the room.

"Oof—sorry!" Molly gasped, tripping on the edge of the carpet.

Sadie grabbed the doorjamb to steady herself, then cast her steel-blue eyes around the room, like a captain setting her bearings at sea. "What have we here?" she asked coldly.

"We knocked, but no one answered—" Molly started to explain.

Sadie put up her hand. "I was out back. Nature called." She gestured toward the small building at the edge of the yard. Molly had assumed it was a shed; now she realized it must be an outhouse.

"Guess I should be used to the snooping O'Connors," Sadie said. "Aren't you going to tell me why you're here?" Molly waited for Todd to speak, but he was frozen like a small child in a game of statues.

When Sadie stalked toward him, her stiff leg dragging, Todd finally moved, edging nervously to the side like a crab. "Excuse us, Cousin Sadie—we didn't mean to barge in."

Molly almost laughed, thinking how tough her brother had sounded a few minutes ago.

"You're excused. I guess you're Todd, all grown up."

"Yes, and this is Kai—"

"We know each other," Sadie interrupted. "Why don't you all sit down? You look as though you're ready to run."

But no one sat or moved.

"Very well," Sadie said. A muscle twitched beneath her eye and a lacy net of wrinkles pulled her mouth into a hard, firm line. "Since you don't choose to talk, I'll have to ask questions. What did you think of the clippings?" she asked Molly.

"I hated them," Molly blurted. She felt the hurt about her mother open up again, like an ugly blister rubbing on her heel. "Was it fun to make me cry? To make me think my mom and dad didn't love each other?" Molly's voice broke. To her surprise, Sadie looked ashamed; she brushed Molly's hand with her cold, dry fingers. Molly shuddered. Was this as close as Sadie could get to saying she was sorry?

"You asked me for information," Sadie reminded her. "Besides, I told you to keep these things to yourself."

"I couldn't!" Molly cried, and jumped when Todd barked, from behind, "Leave my sister alone!"

Sadie's mouth pursed tight with anger, but Todd didn't seem to notice. "I think you owe us an apology," he blurted. "Stealing things that belonged to our mother. What else have you got hidden here?"

Molly watched her brother. His neck and cheeks were mottled and red, and she wondered if he might start throwing things again.

Sadie gripped the back of a chair. Her gnarled hand shook. "I guess we'd better talk." She glanced at Kai and said coldly, "I'm afraid this is family business."

But Molly shook her head. "She's staying. We're all in this together." She grabbed Kai's arm and they stood in a ragged line, Kai holding her breath, Todd shifting uneasily from one foot to the other.

The room was silent for a long time. "Your brother's right," Sadie said at last, speaking directly to Molly, as if they were alone, "I do have something else to show you. Don't go away—I'll be right back."

CHAPTER 17

While Sadie was gone, Todd turned his back on Molly and stood looking out the window. "Are you sure you don't want me to leave?" Kai whispered. Molly shook her head.

In a few minutes, Sadie returned carrying a long, rolled paper tied with string. She lowered herself stiffly into a chair. Amos, the cat, stalked in, complaining and whining, and Sadie drew him into her lap, scratching his ears with her long bony fingers. The cat's belly rumbled with pleasure, and Sadie began to speak.

"It's time to tell you something that's bothered me for years," she said.

The room was so quiet Molly heard the flicker of individual raindrops spattering in the maple leaves outside.

"I blame myself for your mother's death."

164

Molly was stunned. "Why?" she whispered.

"I got her started on some foolishness out west. It's true she went to do geology. But I'm the one who showed her this family tree."

Sadie pushed the cat from her lap and unrolled the document. Inching closer, Kai and Todd stared at the spidery web of names and dates, fanning from a central pair at the top.

"Look, Molly," Kai said, "here's your name and Todd's." They huddled together, forgetting Sadie, and Molly followed Kai's finger to the branch where someone had written: *"Todd O'Connor, b. 1972,"* then Molly's name, with her year of birth, 1974. She and Todd were connected, on the paper, to *"Mark O'Connor, b. 1944,"* and *"Ashley Bell O'Connor, b. 1945."* Yet another hand had added, in pencil, after Ashley's name: "d. 1978."

"I don't understand," Molly said softly. "What does this have to do with Mommy's trip?"

"Bear with me, girl. I've puzzled it through in my mind for ten years, but I've never had to explain it out loud." Sadie turned the paper over. "Here's my own version of the tree, with the people we need to know about."

Molly stole a look at the old woman's face. A thin bead of sweat had formed on her upper lip, and her hands were trembling. As Sadie spread the sheet on the table, Molly suddenly saw a familiar name, five generations back. "Oh, look!" she cried. "Here's Abigail Parker, and Caroline—" She bit her lip, realizing, too late, what she'd said.

"Ha!" Sadie's sharp laugh made them all jump. "So you've been doing some figuring, too." When Molly didn't answer, she snapped, "Very well. We'll go into that later." Her gnarled finger ran along the side of the page. "Abigail and Caroline were sisters. Maybe you know that. From Abigail we got Molly Reed—you see, your name's in the family—Molly, then Constance, then Elizabeth—your grandmother. Then Ashley, that's your side. As for me, Caroline's my ancestor. Caroline, Moses, Jacob—then Sadie. They tended more to boys in that branch." She touched Molly's breastbone with the tip of her finger. "Our ancestors were sisters. And my mother died birthing me. You and I have more in common than you think."

Molly shivered. *Never*, she thought. She'd never be like Sadie, just because the old woman had lost her mother, too.

"Well, that line stopped with me," Sadie continued. "I'm too ornery for most men. Though I always dreamed of children, even put things aside, thinking I'd have them someday."

Molly remembered the spooky drawer full of baby shoes upstairs, and felt a tug of sympathy. She tried to ignore it by studying the genealogy.

"Aren't you going to tell us why you're responsible for her death?" Todd demanded. His arms were crossed over his chest, and he stuck his chin out, as if ready for a fight.

"I'm coming to that," Sadie said sharply. "I told your mother how one branch of our family did things backward: moved west to California during the Gold Rush, then migrated back east when everyone else was still settling the prairies. Ashley got fixated on it. 'You mean we had ancestors in the Gold Rush?' she said. I'll never forget the way her eyes lit up, as if she'd just won the lottery."

Sadie went to the window and rested her hand on the sill. "I thought she could look up old records if she was in the area, see what happened to the people who stayed there. But Ashley wanted more than that. She thought if she was descended from gold miners, it would explain how she turned out so different from everyone in her family. Maybe then her own father—even her husband—would understand her a little better. I never dreamed she'd get so wrought up over it. 'Sadie,' she said to me, just before she left, 'every geologist's a little crazy. We're all prospectors, at heart.'"

Sadie sighed, reached into her apron pocket, and pulled out a wrinkled postcard. "This is the last I heard from her."

Molly glanced at the glossy picture on the front: a restored mining town that looked like a movie set. On the back, her mother had written:

Dear Sadie. Have I got a surprise for you! Our ancestors were more interesting than we imagined. I'll share it all with you when I get home. And I've met the most wonderful man out here. How's the family feud? See you soon. Love —A.

Todd grabbed the card from Molly, read it quickly, and tossed it on the table, as if it were hot. "Why didn't you tell Dad?" he demanded.

"I tried," Sadie said. "But what was there to tell him? That she died chasing after her ancestors? That she'd met a wonderful man? He didn't want to hear any of it."

He still doesn't, Molly thought.

Amos rubbed against Sadie's legs; she scooped him up and ruffled his fur the wrong way until he twisted out of her arms. "After she died, I got suspicious—thinking there was something that lured her there—but I had no proof, except the way she talked about prospecting that one time." She raised her eyebrows at Molly. "Is there something else I should know?"

"No," Todd said firmly, giving his sister a warning look.

Molly glared back at him. "I can tell Sadie what I want."

"What more do you need?" Todd's voice was tight. "Didn't you read the postcard?" He grabbed it and underlined the writing with his thick forefinger. "It's right here, plain as day: *I've met the most wonderful man.* God, Molly, are you blind?"

"No," Sadie said, with a short laugh, "she's not blind. Just stubborn. Like the rest of her family."

Molly glanced at Sadie. Was that a compliment, or an insult?

Todd turned up his hands. Small patches of sweat darkened the front of his T-shirt. "Fine. Have it your way," he said to Molly. "But don't expect me to protect you when Dad comes home. I'm out of this." He grabbed Kai's hand. "Let's split. I took the day off. We might as well enjoy it."

Kai hesitated, her dark eyes pleading with Molly. "We could all go to my house," she said. "I've got a new tape—"

"No thanks," Molly said gently, and when Kai looked worried, she added, "It's OK. You guys go on ahead. Maybe I'll come over later." She knew she wouldn't, but Kai sounded relieved when she said good-bye.

The kitchen door slammed and Sadie said, "I've made your brother angry." Her mouth twitched.

Molly looked her cousin straight in the eye. "I'm glad they've left," she said, "because I know what Mommy wanted to share with you. I know why she went to California."

Sadie rolled up the family tree and tied it carefully with string. "Your turn," she said firmly.

"So you see," Molly said when she was done, "you were right about the woman in the old photograph. She's in the family." Sadie didn't move. "It's not your fault," Molly added. "When Mommy got that letter from Miss Darby, she must have been so excited."

Sadie looked down at her hands. A lonely tear snaked its way over her dry cheek. "Maybe it's time to let the blame rest," she said, smoothing her apron. "If I can." She raised her chin. "What will you do now?"

"I'd like to go there," Molly said, "but I don't know how—it will cost a lot, and my parents will never let me do it."

"Wish I could help you," Sadie said. She swept her arm around the dingy room. "As you can see, I could use a little gold dust myself. Just don't go off without telling me. That's what Ashley did."

"Maybe she wanted to surprise you," Molly said.

Sadie's face lit up for an instant with a tiny smile. "Could be." She handed Molly the family tree. "It's up to you, now."

How can it be up to me? Molly wanted to cry. *I'm only fourteen years old!* But she bit her lip and followed Sadie silently outside.

"What did Mommy mean about the family feud?" Molly asked as the screen door banged behind her.

Sadie frowned. "Your grandpa Sam and I, we fought over your mother. He didn't like her spending time with me. He blamed me for everything—but it wasn't my fault she got going on geology! As soon as she could walk, she was bringing home rocks and bugs—things your grandmother wished she'd keep outside." Sadie smiled, and Molly suddenly imagined her mother—a skinny girl with scraped knees—dumping her treasures on Grand Nan's kitchen table.

"Your grandparents and I stopped talking when Ashley was about Todd's age," Sadie continued. "Later on, Ashley teased us all, begged us to give it up."

"Why didn't you?" Molly asked.

Sadie shrugged. "Too pigheaded, I guess. Come here,

let me show you something." She led Molly slowly around the corner of the house and across the rough lawn in back. Her old shoes drew wet streaks through the long grass. She gestured toward the sagging barn at the corner of the yard. "This farm's been in our family for more than a hundred years. Once, it was one piece of land. My property was part of your grandfather's orchard."

"Really?" Sadie and Grand Nan lived on two parallel roads. Molly had never thought of Sadie's house, perched on the brow of Soldiers' Hill, as having any link with her grandparents' place, nestled in the crook of an ancient apple orchard below.

Sadie limped toward the crumbling stone wall, where the pasture, growing up to pines and hardhack, inched closer to the woods. "There was a farm road here—look, there's still an old path under the maples." Between the trees, two stone walls, about twenty feet apart, snaked down the hill. The land between them had the sunken look of an abandoned roadbed.

"Grand Nan and I were friends as well as cousins," Sadie said. "Somehow, we let Sam put a wedge between us." For a moment, her eyes grew soft. "People say I should sell this place. But I can't. I'll die here, first." Her long, wrinkled hand, mottled with liver spots, rested a moment on Molly's arm.

"Maybe it was wrong to give you the clippings," Sadie said. "Truth is, I'm too old to puzzle this out—but you're not. When I found you snooping, I thought: This girl won't give up until she knows the truth. Will you?"

"No," Molly said with a tiny smile. "That's a promise."
She looked into the woods, dripping with rain. It was
hard to meet Sadie's piercing gaze for long. "If I went
down this old path, would I get to Grand Nan's?"

"Eventually," Sadie said. "Just keep going downhill. I
don't know how clear the trail is, farther down. But it's
not far. Faster than the road, I should think."

Molly climbed up on the wall. "Sadie," she said hesi-
tantly, "did you know I mow lawns for people? If you'd
like, I could cut your grass sometime. For free. It must
be hard, with your sore knee."

She wondered if Sadie would be insulted, but instead,
the old woman nodded. "Thanks. I'd like that." She
waved good-bye, her torn dress and scraggly hair as
unkempt as the hedgerow dividing the yard from the
pasture.

Molly tried to see the overgrown field and tumbled
buildings the way Sadie might, and she felt a shift inside
her. She loves this place, Molly thought. And she loved
my mother, in her own cross way. I wonder what she
thinks of me?

Molly picked her way through the woods, enjoying
the feel of wet brush swishing against her bare legs. For
a while, the trees were thick, but after a few hundred
yards, the land opened up a little and Molly noticed old
gnarled apple trees scattered among the maples. In a few
minutes, she saw the back of her grandmother's house.
Molly hesitated. Blair's car was still in the driveway.
Even though she hadn't seen Grand Nan in a few days,

Molly didn't want to go in. She crept guiltily through the woods at the edge of the yard and ran out to the road, where she jogged down the hill.

Halfway home, Molly passed Kai's driveway. She slowed to a walk, glancing across the Stewarts' lawn at the French doors. Someone—probably Kai and Todd—had left them open to the rain. Molly guessed they were in the family room, where they'd sink down on the Stewarts' deep leather couch and listen to music.

Let's hope that's *all* they do, Molly thought. She pictured them kissing. It was easy to imagine Kai puckering her lips and fluttering her eyes until the lashes gently covered her black eyes—Molly had watched her perform this way in front of a mirror many times. But Todd? What did she see in *him?* Molly ran until she reached her driveway half a mile farther down the road.

Before she went up the hill, she opened the mailbox and sifted through a stack of junk mail and bills. On the bottom of the pile was a cardboard packet addressed to Molly that said, in bold letters, EXPRESS MAIL. OVERNIGHT DELIVERY. Molly forgot about Todd and Kai; she raced across the bridge, slid down the bank, and huddled under the rough timbers to tear open the parcel.

A photo fell out into her lap: a color closeup of two boys about Todd's age, one a blond holding a shovel, the other—dark-skinned with jet-black hair cut into a short brush—was brandishing some kind of shallow pan. One look at his smile convinced Molly he must be Ramon. He was wearing cutoff shorts, a T-shirt with torn sleeves, and a single gleaming earring. "You're not a nerd," Molly giggled. She turned the picture over. *"That's me, with Larry, my panning partner,"* Ramon had scrawled. *"I'm the dark one."*

Molly studied him. If he'd been right in front of her, she knew she'd have to look away. That kind of saucy gaze in a boy always made her shy. But now she could stare at his eyes, trying to find the point where the black pupils stopped and the dark iris began. She could whisper, "Hey, Ramon," run a finger gently over his arm and imagine how his skin would feel. And what did he mean, his "panning partner?" Did they look for gold together? Molly opened the note he'd enclosed, a quick scrawl on a torn piece of paper.

> *Here's yours truly. This is the way I look when I'm not under Miss Darby's nose. Relaxed, huh? We were hoping for a big strike that day, but all we found were some old bottles.*
>
> *Here's another letter. I think this might be the last one—I've searched all of Darby's files for that year. Looks important—I'll send it Express. What shall I do next? Give me a call.*
>
> *Love, Ramon*
>
> P.S. *Don't forget I want a picture of you.*

" 'Love!' " Molly squealed. She read the letter twice. When she opened the folded photocopy, it started to rain harder. Molly stuffed it under her shirt and ran for the house.

The kitchen was quiet. The old floorboards creaked as Molly went to the table and opened the last piece of paper. She recognized Abigail Parker's handwriting immediately. The letter was dated "July, 1870," and began:

Dearest Caroline,

I was so sad to hear of Jacob's death. You must be shattered. I know how lost I would feel if anything ever happened to Matthew.

We're planning to come stay the winter with you. Don't argue; the change will be wonderful, and it's been five years since we were together. We'll arrive before snow flies and come home in the spring. Who knows, maybe you'll want to come back here with us?

Your niece is tall and healthy; Molly is a strong-willed girl, like all the Parker women.

Molly stopped reading. This was the Molly she'd seen in the family tree. *"A strong-willed girl"*— Molly grinned and returned to the letter. Abigail went on to give her sister more sympathy and to discuss details of the journey east, which she planned to make by rail for the first time. Then she said:

Caroline, you know I don't trust mountain travel. Perhaps it's the memories I have from

*our wagon trip so long ago. I'm sure you will
laugh and say trains are safer than oxen, but I
must tell you this. If something happens to us,
I want you to know there are treasures and
family keepsakes hidden near my cabin. I've
kept them buried beneath the roots of the little
apple tree we planted on the southwest corner.
You follow the road down to the ravine. Go to
the place where everyone mines—you'll see; the
creek makes a wide curve, and the banks are
often busy with miners. Our cabin is about 400
yards downstream, where the land opens up a
little.*

    *There, now I've told you, and let's pray you
never need to climb down here to find it! I'll see
you before you know it. In haste,*

                Your loving sister, Abigail.

    Molly nearly screamed. "I've got everything now!"
she cried. "It's like having a map—" She stopped and
took a deep breath. It wasn't quite complete—there was
no mention of Kenton Mine, the name on the crude sign
behind Abigail in the old photograph, nothing to say if
her cabin really was on Kanaka Creek. But I'm getting
closer, Molly thought.

    "Ramon," she breathed, hugging herself, "you've got
just one more job to do. And then somehow, some way,
I'm going to go out there."

CHAPTER 18

For the next two days, Todd and Molly avoided each other, keeping a stony silence when they met at the dinner table until Blair, exasperated, snapped, "Come on, you two—whatever it is, drop it." After that, they spoke politely, but when Blair asked about their visit to Sadie's, they clammed up completely.

It was Friday before Molly worked up the nerve to call Ramon, and even then she put it off all day. It was hot and sunny, the first of July. Molly mowed two lawns, went to the lake, then waited at home until Blair finally emerged from the darkroom to go into town. When the house was empty, Molly sat by the phone, twisting the scrap of paper where Kai had written Ramon's number. Finally, she dialed, holding her breath while the phone rang three, then four times.

"Nevada City Historical Society."

"Ramon," Molly said, relieved. "It's Molly O'Connor. From Vermont."

"Hello, Molly-from-Vermont. Afraid I wouldn't remember you?" When Molly didn't answer he said, "Well, I'm glad you called. Perfect timing—Darby's gone to the post office."

"I liked your picture," Molly said, finding her voice.

"So when will I see the real you?" he asked.

"Soon," Molly promised, although she didn't really know how she would manage it. "Listen, can you do me one more favor?"

"Anything."

Molly's stomach danced. She clutched the phone to her ear. "There was once a place called Kenton Mine—it might have been on Kanaka Creek, near Allegheny—"

"If it exists, I'll uncover it," Ramon boasted. "Anything else?"

"That letter you sent was great," Molly said. "If we can figure out where Abigail Parker lived, we could dig up the gold."

"We?" Ramon asked. "This sounds more and more promising. When should I expect you?"

But Molly couldn't answer. Her ears had caught a familiar sound. "Oh, no—my dad's home. Listen, I have to run." She said good-bye quickly and sauntered out to the porch, trying to calm her heart. When the truck came to a trembling stop in front of the house, Molly walked casually down the steps and leaned on her father's door as he cut the engine.

"Whoo-ee! Home at last!" her father shouted. He opened the door and gave her a quick hug.

Molly stared at the clutter of Styrofoam cups, greasy plates, and candy wrappers on the floor of the cab. "Looks like you lived on junk food."

"You said it." Her father climbed out and arched his back until it popped. "Endless days—we worked over-time, to get out early. Worth it, though. We won't have to worry about money for a while." He opened the tailgate. "Want to help me with my bags—what'd you do all week?"

"It's a long story," Molly said nervously, but she'd already lost his attention. His eyes drifted across the tall grass to the woodpile; she felt him itching to start mowers, sharpen his chain saw.

"Looks like there's plenty to do here," her father said, scowling. "No one's cut the grass—and where's Blair?"

"She went to the store." Molly glanced at her father and felt her stomach tighten. *Now*, she told herself. Tell him now, while no one's home.

But he was on his way to the kitchen, where Molly watched him drain two glasses of water, one after the other, then lower his head sideways to the faucet to splash his face. "Dusty job, this week. Lots of blasting."

Molly followed her father back to the porch. "Guess I'll unload my tools," he said.

Molly winced. She wasn't ready to deal with the broken window and its temporary cover of torn plastic. "Dad, wait a sec. I have to tell you something."

At last he gave her his full attention. His eyes, lit with the pleasure of being home, were a warm auburn, like the cherry boards he most enjoyed working with. "What's up?"

Molly plunged in. "I found out a lot about Mommy while you were gone. I think I know why she went to California. And I've read—about the man in the truck."

"What the—" Her father clutched his belt buckle, as if Molly had punched him. "Didn't I tell you to leave these things alone?"

"I couldn't," Molly said, and she started to cry.

"Oh, boy." Her father paced the length of the porch, kicking a soccer ball aside. He tugged his mustache, rubbed the back of his neck, then whirled to face her. "All right. You win." He dropped onto the porch swing. "Come on, sit down."

When Molly joined him, he pushed at the wooden flooring to set the swing in motion. The rusty chains creaked. "I always hoped you and Todd would never have to hear about this," he said at last. "I guess that was foolish of me. It's something I never understood. I thought Ashley and I had a good thing—" He swallowed hard, then stood up and went to the porch railing, facing the hills.

"Ever since you started asking questions, I've been thinking about your mother, and how I must have made life hard for her. I hated it when she traveled. I thought she should study geology here in Vermont, but she said it had all been done." He gripped a post with one hand, hunched his shoulders, and spoke to the trees in the yard, as if he'd forgotten Molly was there.

"We fought like crazy every time she went away. I knew she loved you kids, and I thought she loved me —so why would she want to leave?" He turned to look at Molly, as if she might have the answer. Molly's stomach was churning; she braced her feet against the porch floor to keep the swing from moving.

"She said her work was like a drug, she couldn't give it up," Molly's father said. "She'd get these urges to run, and I'd try to catch hold of her, keep her at home—it always made things worse."

As his words spilled out, Molly realized that her father, like Sadie, had kept everything bottled up tight since the accident.

"I thought, deep down, she really needed me," he said. "Once, she even said I was her anchor—"

"Stop!" Molly interrupted. She couldn't stand the way his voice kept breaking. "It's not your fault that she went out there. Sadie told Mommy about some ancestors in the Gold Rush—"

"Sadie!" her father exploded. "Leave that witch out of this."

"She's not a witch!" Molly cried. "She's a lonely old lady."

Her father's face was red, and Molly could tell he was trying to control his temper. "Listen, Mol," he said carefully, "Sadie wanted your mother to look up some old relatives. Ashley humored her, but that's not why she went. She needed to study certain rock formations, and to get away from me—and she did that," he said bitterly. "Got away, for good." Molly could almost feel the pain close his throat, the way it was tightening another notch around her own heart.

"I'm sorry, Mol. No kid wants to think about her parents having hard times, or being unfaithful. But it happens. After she died, I wondered if she'd known that man for years."

"No way!" Molly cried. "She was looking for gold—and I'm going to California to find it. *Then* you'll be sorry."

She jumped up, pushing the swing so hard it smacked the wall and lurched wildly into her leg. Her father grabbed her, gripping her shoulders with his wide fingers and shaking her until she felt her backbone jangle into her skull.

"No one in this family goes to that place in California, ever again," he hissed. "Do you understand me?"

"Let me go!" Molly cried, twisting away. "That hurts!" She pounded on his chest with her fists. "You don't care how this feels to me. You never have. But you can't keep me here. I'll run away. You don't even want to know the truth!"

"You're damned right!" her father shouted, shaking her again. "Did it ever occur to you that I don't want to mess up another marriage?"

"Mark—what are you doing?" Blair came running across the grass, her hair disheveled, her face white with fear. Neither Molly nor her father had heard the car arrive—it was perched at the top of the hill with the door open. Blair stumbled up the steps and grabbed Molly from behind, pulling her close. Molly sobbed desperately, her shoulders heaving, but she wouldn't take her eyes off her father.

Blair clasped her hands around Molly's waist. "What's going on here?" she demanded, her voice trembling next to Molly's ear.

Mark O'Connor stepped toward Molly but she cringed back against her stepmother, letting Blair's small body form a solid wall at her back. When her father tried to cup Molly's chin in his rough hand, she twisted her face to the side.

"Molly, forgive me," he said hoarsely. "I don't know what happened—when you said 'California,' I lost it. I thought maybe—" He swallowed. "I was afraid you'd be like her. Running off. I don't want to lose you, too." His eyes were wet when he turned to Blair, begging her to understand. "I'm sorry, hon. I hate to drag you into all this stuff."

Blair released her hold on Molly's waist. "It's never far away for any of us," she said in a grim voice. "Don't you know that? Now Molly's found a way out, but you're such a stubborn fool, you can't even *see*."

Molly glanced from Blair to her father, trying to still her shaking body. Would her parents split up? If they do, it's my fault, Molly decided.

"Why don't you drop this stupid pain." Blair's voice was tight. "Did you ever think what it might be like for me, living in a house with a ghost?"

Molly's father groaned and sank onto the porch steps, holding his head. Molly wanted to run away, but her sneakers were welded to the wet boards and her hand was glued to Blair's. After a long time, her father looked up, his eyes red and swollen. "What's this about gold?" he asked.

Molly felt the tension ease. Her father sounded a little more like himself. She propped herself against the railing, wiping her nose with her sleeve. At first, she couldn't speak. Her voice was as halting and broken as a tiny child who's cried herself into a stupor. Finally, she was able to tell him what she had learned in a few weeks, confessing everything—including the way she'd stolen his letter from Ramon, snooped around at Sadie's, and called California long distance, running up a phone bill. "And I smashed the window in your shop, too," she said, starting to cry again.

"Easy, Mol." Her father stood up and stepped toward her. "I never knew how much this meant to you. I didn't think about what a girl misses when her mother dies." He hugged her gingerly, as if she were made of delicate paper. "One thing's for sure," he said, "you inherited her determination."

Molly let her tears fall until his T-shirt was wet against her cheek. Blair put a hand on her shoulder. "I didn't realize you'd put so many pieces together," she said. "Is that what was in those letters?"

Molly nodded.

"Let's start this conversation again," her father said,

when Molly had pulled away. "Tell me why you want to go out west."

"To find out what really happened," Molly said simply.

"What if you wind up with an ugly picture of your mother?"

"I won't," Molly said, although she knew he could be right.

"And how did you plan to get there?"

Molly swallowed hard and looked down the hill at the sheep. Standing apart from the rest of the flock was Lotty, Molly's three-year-old ewe. This spring, she'd given birth to female twins that had her fine fleece and slightly startled face.

"I could sell Lotty and her babies," Molly whispered.

Her father whistled, a long, slow note of surprise. "All right—she's yours. That might pay for your fare one way. What about the rest?"

He's going to let me go, Molly thought, and her stomach turned over. "I'm earning lots of money, mowing lawns," she said in a near whisper. "I could do some baby-sitting, even though I hate it." She smiled weakly. "I'd have plenty by the end of the summer."

Her father tugged his mustache. "I'll have to think about it," he said at last. "You can't go alone."

"She won't." Blair took Molly's hand. "We're in this together—if that's all right with you, Mol."

Molly shrugged. "Sure," she said, and then added, when she saw a tiny flicker of pain cross Blair's face, "I mean yes. That would be great." Her voice trembled again, and she swallowed hard.

Mark shook his head. "That's not right. You can't go looking for my first wife."

"I'm not," Blair said. "I'm helping Molly. It's been painful for her, and frankly, you haven't made it any easier."

Molly's father winced. "I can see that."

Blair took hold of Molly's hair and began to braid it, absently flicking the strands from side to side. "You told me on the phone you'd bring home big money this summer," Blair said. "When I get paid for my cover photo, I'll have enough for a plane ticket for my-self. And who knows what pictures I might take out there?"

Molly's father crossed his arms and leaned against the railing. His eyes were empty. "I see. I didn't realize you had this all worked out ahead of time."

"We didn't!" Molly protested.

"She's telling the truth." Blair tucked the short braid into Molly's shirt collar. "This is the first time we've ever talked about it." She sat on the railing and took Mark's large hand in her two small ones, turning it over and tracing the thick calluses with one finger. "No matter what she finds out, it will be good for all of us," Blair said softly. "It's time to spread the dark secrets out in the sunshine."

They heard someone singing. Todd, on his way home from work, appeared on the brow of the hill. His song trailed away when he saw them. "Hey, Dad," he said casually, avoiding Molly's eyes, "welcome home."

Mark O'Connor tried to smile. "Thanks. It's nice *someone's* glad to see me."

No one spoke until Molly said, "Dad knows."

Todd looked quickly at his father. "I told her to stay out of it," he muttered.

Molly could have hit him. "So why'd you go to Sadie's?" she challenged. He flinched, but didn't answer. Molly felt her father's eyes on her back, and sensed Blair waiting, holding her breath. "You can pretend you're not interested," Molly said. "I don't care. I'll go to California alone."

"What—you're going out there?"

Molly saw the fear in her brother's eyes. Was he afraid of what she'd find? She took a deep breath to keep her voice steady. "You could come, too."

Todd's face snapped toward their father. "You're letting her go?"

He shrugged. "I'm not sure I can say no."

Todd pulled off his shirt, balled it up, and used it like a towel on his face. His freckled chest was streaked with sweat and his cheeks, when they appeared from under his shirt, were ruddy and tan. For a second, Molly forgave Kai for liking him; she could almost call him handsome, though she would never admit it to anyone.

"I'd better stay here. I'd just wreck it for you." Todd looked quickly at Molly. "I'm sorry—I *want* to believe your idea, Mol, but I just can't."

"That's OK," Molly said sadly.

"Blair will go with her," their father explained. "You can work in New Hampshire with me while they're gone."

Everyone was silent. Molly felt their eyes on her, and realized they were all waiting for her to say something. What am I *doing?* she thought, suddenly feeling panicked. She ran to the fence, leaped over, and tore through the pasture, tripping on hummocks of grass, as frightened as the sheep scattering in front of her. Blair called out, but Molly didn't stop until she was halfway to the river, where she flopped under the wide maple, panting. In a few minutes, Lotty trotted over to her, nuzzling Molly's chest with her nose while Molly wove her fingers into the long, sticky fleece.

"Dear Lotty," she whispered, "remember when you were born? Dad had to swing you around his head to get your heart going." Molly's eyes filled as she thought of that night: her father standing in the barnyard with snow swirling in the security light, the lamb, with its tiny legs splayed out, whirling in a blurred circle around his head. "Your mama didn't like you," Molly said to Lotty, "so I gave you bottles. How can I sell you?"

As if she understood, the ewe darted away, her round udder swinging between her legs. This is the summer of broken things, Molly thought. She glanced back at the house. Her family seemed shattered, like the window in the shop, the pieces glinting in the sawdust on the floor. She could fix the shop window, but who would mend her family?

It began to rain again. As water dripped rhythmically through the massive canopy of the maple tree, it seemed to say: *Ra-mon*. The cinch around her chest loosened a little and she opened her eyes. There must be a way, she thought, and the words of her next letter floated into her head, as if they'd been hovering in the damp air around her:

Dear Ramon. I'm coming to California.

She'd tell him her plans, and sign it, *Love, Molly*.

CHAPTER 19

On a Sunday morning in August, Molly sat in the back of her family's station wagon, watching the landscape change from green mountains, soft in the summer haze, to cluttered suburbs. As the Boston skyline came in sight, she thought about the last five weeks, which had passed in a blur of yard work and baby-sitting, short swims at the lake and long calls with Ramon. Every night, she'd crossed another day off the calendar. On Fridays, she'd passed her earnings on to Blair, adding them to the money she'd clutched in her hand when the cattle truck lurched down her driveway, carrying Lotty and her babies away.

And now they were leaving. Last night, Molly had rushed from Grand Nan's to Sadie's to Kai's, saying good-bye, hardly hearing their good wishes. She knew

Kai and Todd would spend hours together while she was gone. She knew Grand Nan was puzzled and confused by what Molly was doing, and that Sadie was half serious when she'd said, "Don't come back unless you find something." But Molly couldn't react. She felt as if she were moving along in a movie with the sound turned off. Even the wet, sticky feeling of her shirt, plastered to the seat of the car by the heat, couldn't convince Molly this was real. She pinched her leg, hard, then glanced at the back of her father's head. He'd hardly spoken since they'd left home, and his eyebrows were drawn into a narrow line as he focused on the stream of rush-hour traffic, pouring toward the tunnel. Molly knew he still didn't want her to go, but it was too late now. A rush of yellow tiles and emergency phones whipped past their windows, the car bolted into daylight, and then, straight ahead, the airport control tower loomed on twin concrete pillars.

Molly opened her backpack for the tenth time, checking to make sure she had everything. Nestled among her books were the letters, the daguerreotype, the clippings, and a copy of the family tree. Molly's stomach rose with a plane lifting ponderously from the runway beside them.

Inside the airport, they checked their bags and found their gate. When the ticket agent called their flight, Molly's parents kissed each other twice and then, as Blair fussed with her bag, looking for their tickets, Molly faced her father. "Good-bye, Dad."

He pulled her close, but let go quickly. His eyes were sad. "Take it easy. I hope you find what you want—but don't get your hopes up."

"I'll be fine," Molly said, although her feelings were jangling like the beepers on the little carts that whizzed through the terminal, carrying older passengers to their planes. The ticket agent opened the door to the skyway, Molly gripped Blair's arm, and they were swallowed up by the crowd.

In the air, Molly pressed her face to the window until her breath fogged the plastic. She hadn't flown since she was little, and had forgotten the pressing sensation of lift-off, the sudden speed followed by unnatural calm. The clouds outside were stacked up like meringues. Molly imagined she could reach out, scoop up a bite, and let it slither down her throat like ice cream.

When the landscape became an endless pattern of square fields intersected by roads, Molly put her head back and closed her eyes. Today, she'd meet Ramon. And then what? Molly slept, and woke when Blair tugged at her sleeve.

"The Rockies," Blair said. Molly watched the mountains sail past beneath them, followed by miles of gray-brown desert, flecked with sage. She tried to imagine her ancestors winding through that bleak landscape to scale the barren cliffs beyond.

In Sacramento, they rented a car. Molly held the road map open on her lap, guiding Blair around the city and into the foothills of the Sierras. They passed sloping, tawny fields, then drove past orchards and smaller farms. As the road narrowed, Molly's stomach lurched with every curve, and she shoved her hands under her legs to keep them from twitching.

When they crossed a bridge and pulled up at the bottom of Nevada City's main street, Molly stared up the sloping hill at the colored houses and stores, some with gingerbread curlicues over the eaves. A few cars hugged the sidewalk, and small clumps of tourists wandered in and out of shops, clutching plastic bags and ice-cream cones. Signs with old-fashioned lettering hung over some of the stores.

"This is a city?" Molly said in disbelief.

"Maybe it was once," Blair said. "Or maybe they had grand plans that fell through. It's not much bigger than Griswold now, is it?" She turned off the engine and they stepped out of the air-conditioned car. Molly lifted her hair off her neck. The hot, dry air tickled her nostrils. She licked her lips, stretched her arms, then froze. Blair was leaning into the back, pulling her cameras out of their bag.

"Blair!" Molly hissed. "Don't carry those. We'll look like tourists!"

Blair laughed. "Molly, we *are* tourists. But I'll stick the smaller one in my purse if it makes you feel better." She fussed with her gear for a minute, hid her camera bag under the seat, and locked the car. "Well," she said, turning to Molly, "this is your trip. What shall we do first?"

No more daydreams, Molly thought. She was here, in California, on a sunny day in August. And somewhere nearby was Ramon. Maybe in the next building. Molly bent to look in the mirror beside the car door, hastily twitching her hair off her face. "I look awful!" she cried. "I'm a mess!"

"No, you're not," Blair said. "But here, take my comb, if you're worried." She dug in her deep bag until she found it, then watched while Molly combed out the tangles. "I take it we're going to see Ramon?" Blair asked.

Molly stared at her stepmother. Blair's hair was escaping from its pins at the back of her head, and her purple shirt was wrinkled from the drive. In spite of the heat, her skin was a pale white, almost translucent. Blair winced. "Do I look that terrible?" she asked. "Here, give me the comb."

When she finished, she winked at Molly. They both laughed, and Molly gripped Blair's arm. "I'm so nervous!" Molly cried. "What if he thinks I'm a jerk?"

"Then we'll know he's a dud," Blair said. "Come on. Maybe someone in that shop across the street can direct us to the Historical Society."

They went into a small, cool store that seemed to sell a bit of everything: plastic packets labeled FOOL YOUR FRIENDS WITH FOOL'S GOLD were stacked inside mining pans. A bulging rack full of maps and postcards sat on the counter above tubs of ice cream.

"Two cones," Blair said to the shopkeeper before Molly even had to beg. "Vanilla fudge for me. What do you want, Mol?"

"Mocha chip," Molly said quickly. As the woman dug

into a cardboard barrel Molly added, "Where's the Historical Society?"

The woman peered at Molly through thick glasses, tinted pink. "Just up the street on the right," she said. "But it's closed, Sundays. Anything particular you're looking for? We've got books on the area."

"Oh—no thanks," Molly said. "That's OK." She took her cone and slipped outside before the woman could ask more questions. Blair joined her and they walked slowly up the hill, licking their cones eagerly and peering into shop windows, until they reached a small, frame building set back from the road. A short, iron fence separated the tiny yard from the street and a sign hung on the locked gate: NEVADA CITY HISTORICAL SOCIETY AND MUSEUM. OPEN MONDAY THROUGH FRIDAY, NOON TO FIVE. SATURDAY 10–2.

Molly swallowed the last bite of her cone and licked her lips. Had her mother stood here, on this same spot, before deciding to go in? Molly looked at her watch. "Eight thirty? How come it's so late?"

"It's only five thirty here," Blair said. "Look, there's a sentry asleep on the porch."

"Where?" Molly saw a flicker of movement; someone was slumped in the shadows. The person stretched, stood up, and stepped into the sunshine. Molly's stomach plunged. She glanced at Blair but her stepmother had moved up the street, suddenly captivated by the display in the gift shop next door.

"Molly?" The boy was lanky and tall, with dusky, olive

skin. He wore a bright yellow T-shirt with the sleeves rolled to the shoulders, tight jeans, and dark glasses. He jumped off the porch, strolled across the yard, and stepped over the fence.

Molly still hadn't said anything. Didn't her voice work anymore? She could almost hear Kai hiss, *Say something, you goof.* Molly opened her mouth, closed it, and feeling like a fool, finally croaked, "Ramon?"

He pulled off his glasses, twirling them with one hand. His eyes were coal black, much darker than she'd imagined.

"That's me," Ramon said. "Did you come alone?"

"Uh, no." Molly remembered Blair and felt her limbs and brain start to thaw. She was surprised to find she could actually wave to Blair, who had crossed the street. "My stepmother's over there," she said, trying to swallow a nervous laugh. "Were you asleep?"

"Afraid so. I've been waiting—I didn't know when you'd get here." He smiled, then surprised her by leaning closer and saying in a husky voice she hadn't heard on the phone, "I loved the pictures. But you're much better in real life."

Something hot pulsed near the base of Molly's spine and surged up through her belly. When Blair arrived and introduced herself to Ramon, Molly was red and speechless again. Her stepmother rescued her, saying, "You two are in charge. Ramon, what do you suggest? Where shall we begin?"

"At my house." Ramon ran his fingers through his

dark hair. "Rosa—that's my mom—is expecting you for dinner."

"Oh no—we couldn't do that—" Blair protested, but Ramon put up his hand.

"Sorry. You don't know Rosa. When she says you're doing something, you do it. She's made a Mexican meal, in your honor. It may sear your tongue, but it will fill you up." Without looking back, he hurried down the street, and Molly and Blair set off behind him, almost trotting to keep up.

Ramon lived on a side street a few blocks from the foot of the hill. He sauntered just ahead of them until they reached his house, a small stucco building with a red tile roof. "When Mama saw this one, she had to have it," Ramon said, taking them through a long, narrow yard. "It's the only Spanish-style place in town." They skirted plastic tricycles and a swing set. The front door was open. As they went in, three little girls with black pigtails clattered down the stairs, pushed past them, and stood in an anxious huddle outside, giggling and holding hands.

"Maria! Christine! Jamila!" Ramon scolded. "Come say hello to our guests." But the girls turned and darted away, their skirts flapping around their knees.

"Sorry they're so rude," Ramon apologized.

Blair laughed. "They're just shy, like the rest of us."

Ramon grinned at Molly, then led them into a bright, square kitchen. His mother came to meet them with her hands out. She was a short woman with a round face, a long thick braid, and eyes as dark and dancing as Ramon's. She dusted flour from her hands, greeting them eagerly.

"I'm Rosa Rodriguez. So glad to meet you. And I hope you're staying for dinner?"

Molly took a deep breath. The mixed fragrance of chili powder, melted cheese, and pungent sauces tickled her nose. Blair laughed. "Everything smells so delicious. How could we say no?"

"Good, good." Rosa Rodriguez smiled. "I was just making sopaipillas—Mexican honey biscuits—they're my specialty. Ramon's told us so much about you, Molly. We're glad to meet you at last."

Molly glanced nervously at Ramon, and Rosa Rodriguez laughed. "Nothing bad, don't worry. Except I can see you're even prettier than we thought. Excuse me," she added quickly, "I'm embarrassing you both now, I see. We need some drinks for dinner—go to the store, the two of you, and get us some juice. Blair, you can help me here." As she was talking, her hands were already back at work, kneading a ball of thick dough on the kitchen table. "Scoot," she said, smiling. "I'm sure you have lots to talk about."

Do we? Molly wondered nervously. She followed Ramon to the sidewalk. It was all so much easier on the phone. When Ramon suddenly stopped walking, Molly nearly bumped into him.

"Well," he said, glancing at her, "where do we start?"

"I don't know." Molly felt empty. How did she ever get into this?

"What are you thinking?" Ramon asked.

"That I'm tired," Molly hedged. She wasn't ready to let Ramon into her thoughts. "Your mother was so friendly," she added, to change the subject. "Just inviting us for dinner, when she doesn't even know us."

Ramon smiled and cocked his head to the side, reminding Molly of some dark, inquisitive bird. "Dad says that's why he likes California—it's not so formal. He says people back east are always waiting to be introduced to someone, but out west, we just plunge right in. Think you could do that while you're here?"

Molly flushed. "Maybe."

"What about the gold?" Ramon asked. They were walking side by side now and Molly matched her quick gait to his easy, long strides. She noticed how his head was a few inches above her own, how his earring caught the sunlight and his dark hair gleamed. He's really something, Kai, she caught herself thinking, and grinned.

"What's so funny?"

Molly blushed. "My friend Kai wondered if you were as cute as your picture."

"Oh?" Ramon stopped and crossed his arms, turning to face her on the sidewalk. "So what will you tell her?"

Molly laughed. "To tell you the truth, I hate that word. *Cute.* It's a word for babies, or your little sisters. They're cute."

"Ha! You should live with them. So what would you call me, if I'm not cute?" Ramon challenged.

Molly looked away. "I'm not sure," she stammered.

Ramon scuffed his toes as they began walking again. "Maybe I can help you. How about 'handsome as the devil,' or 'a crazy nerd', or—" He took a deep breath, raised one arm high, and suddenly turned two cart-wheels on the sidewalk. A loose cascade of change spilled from his pockets.

Molly laughed, and scrambled to grab the spinning dimes and quarters. When Ramon stood up, his face dark, she laughed. "I think the word for you might be 'outrageous.' "

"Whatever you say."

They were passing a small park where a tree spread wide, low arms over a sandbox and an iron bench. Ramon suddenly grabbed her hand. "Come on," he said, tugging her gently, "let's sit for a minute."

Molly couldn't look at him, not when she could feel his smooth palm and short, square fingers, cool against her own. She followed him to the bench and sat down, relieved when he dropped her hand and picked up a stick. He started to draw squiggling lines in the dust.

"Our treasure map," he teased.

Molly glanced at him, then turned away. *Handsome as the devil is right*, she thought. She'd never met anyone like Ramon. Her thoughts began to wander and she jumped, startled, when Ramon's hand touched her knee.

"Are you OK?" he asked.

"Sorry," Molly said, "I'm just thinking. I do that a lot. My family's always bugging me, telling me to wake up."

Ramon laughed. "*My* family wishes I'd shut up. But I don't know how else to behave. Seems like I only think when my mouth is running. Like now. I'm thinking you seem shy, but when you talk, you're really"—he hesitated—"direct."

Molly studied her sneakers. A soft, red dust covered the toes. She wasn't used to having someone talk to her about herself—not outside her family. "Let's figure out what we're going to do."

"OK." Ramon settled back against the bench and threw one arm casually across the back. Molly held herself still, not daring to relax against his arm, not wanting to pull away. But Ramon didn't seem to notice, and he didn't stay still for long. His knees began to bounce, then he tapped out a tune on the bench. "First, we'll see Sam Fry, the man who wrote the newspaper articles about your mother. He runs a diner called Pauline's. Named it after his cat."

Molly laughed. "Really?"

"Yeah. There are some weird people in this town."

"Sounds like Griswold," Molly said, thinking of Sadie. "Maybe we could fix him up with my crazy cousin."

"Right. Anyway, he still remembers about—the accident," Ramon said.

Molly heard the way his voice hesitated over those words. *The accident.* Molly had managed to put all that out of her mind, but now it came slithering back, like a snake sliding out from under a woodpile.

"Then what?" Molly asked, feeling the long day wash over her. She yawned and let herself lean back slowly until she felt the gentle press of Ramon's arm against her shoulders.

"Then—I don't know. It's up to you, I guess," he said. "I called the county clerk's office about Abigail Parker, but their records don't go back that far. And Sam Fry's never heard about the Kenton Mine, but I told him about you. What I knew so far, that is."

He grinned, inched sideways, and cupped his fingers gently around Molly's shoulder. Then one of his knees began to bounce and jiggle; he jumped up and said, "Come on. We'd better go to the store. Rosa will wonder where we are."

When they arrived at the Rodriguez house, carrying the drinks, the kitchen was full of noise and people. In a daze, Molly met Ramon's father, a tall quiet man with a bony face, and a blond boy who perched on a kitchen stool by the door, reading a comic.

"This is Larry," Ramon said, waving at his friend. Molly recognized his face from the snapshot.

"Once in a while, we remember Larry doesn't live here," Rosa Rodriguez said with a laugh. "Then we send him home." Her dark eyes flashed. "Ramon, set the table, please."

When they sat down to eat, Molly felt enveloped in warmth. The hot, spicy chiles rellenos slid down her throat, followed by the sweet sopaipillas. She was quiet while Ramon's sisters jumped up and down from the table, his mother laughed and passed hot dishes, and Ramon and Larry bantered with one another. Her eyes drooped; she leaned back in her chair and yawned, feeling a smile spread inside.

Near the end of dinner, Ramon jolted her back to life when he said, "What's happening tomorrow? I'm taking some time off. Where shall we start?"

Molly couldn't answer, and Rosa Rodriguez chided, "Come on, Ramon, can't you see the girl's exhausted? Give her some peace. Let it wait until morning."

Molly nodded, grateful. Ramon's mother was right. In the morning, she'd be ready to make plans, to think about finding the mine, maybe even talk to the newspaper reporter. But for tonight, she'd enjoy this dreamy, slightly numb state.

Soon, Blair said it was time to go. Molly thanked Ramon's parents and followed her stepmother to the car. She was asleep on the front seat before Blair had slipped the key into the ignition.

CHAPTER 20

When Molly woke the next morning, Blair was sitting on the end of her bed, winding a new role of film into her camera.

Molly groaned. "What time is it?"

"Seven. I couldn't sleep, because of the time change. Roll over, if you want."

Molly shifted in bed, trying to find a flat place in the lumpy mattress.

"Doze a little longer," Blair whispered. "I'll be back in a while."

"No—wait for me. I've got to get going, and find out where the mine is." Molly jumped out of bed, pulling clean clothes from her bag. She barely remembered arriving at the motel the night before. The cabin was set back from the road under tall pines, and the motel units next door were empty. Molly didn't want to stay there alone.

While Molly dressed, Blair explored the tiny kitchen, opening drawers and cupboards. "Nothing here but coffee and tea—let's go into town and look for a breakfast place. We'll cook here tomorrow."

"Ramon told me about a diner called Pauline's," Molly remembered, yawning.

"Great," Blair said. They were in the car before Molly realized she might see Sam Fry there. And then what?

They drove into town and circled up and down the main street until they spotted a parking lot, already filled with trucks. A low, silver diner sat on cinder blocks and an unlit, neon sign read PAULINE'S.

"This must be it," Molly said, and followed Blair into a warm, steamy room smelling of coffee. She slid onto a stool, read the menu quickly, and glanced around. The diner was filled with men; the tool belts around their waists reminded Molly of her father.

She listened to the clatter of saucers and watched the cook, a big man with a gleaming, bald head, move from the grill to the toaster to the refrigerator and back again, his wide hands in constant motion as he broke eggs, flipped pancakes, and poured coffee. He caught Molly's eyes in the mirror that ran the length of the diner, smiled, and waved his spatula. "What can I get you?" he asked, whirling easily in spite of his bulk.

Molly and Blair ordered eggs and homemade muffins. The man next to them unfolded a crinkled bill from his pocket and said, "Well, Sam—another good day?"

The cook nodded, keeping his back to them. "Always a good day at Pauline's," he said.

Sam. Molly licked her lips. Was this Sam Fry? Who else could it be? When he brought her plate, she glanced quickly at his face, long and oval like an egg. He didn't look like a newspaper reporter, but still— Molly ate her breakfast slowly and drank her juice. Groups of men got up to leave, and the room grew quiet. Sun filtered through the windows and the waitress, who'd been rushing from the sink to the booths, sank onto an empty stool and lit a cigarette.

"Isn't it always like this," the cook said to her. "They all come at once, and then it's empty." He wiped his face with the corner of his apron. "Excuse me, ladies," he said, smiling at Molly and Blair, "not quite empty." He put their check on the counter and asked, "More coffee?"

"Please," Blair said, pushing her cup toward him.

Molly heard Ramon's voice inside her, saying *plunge right in*. "Excuse me," she said, clearing her throat, "are you Mr. Fry?"

Blair's head swiveled in astonishment, but Molly kept her eyes on the big man's face.

"Most folks just call me Sam." He cocked his head and smiled. His eyes were a deep blue, and they twinkled.

"Ramon Rodriguez told me about you," Molly said in a near whisper. "I need—to ask you something."

He tipped his head forward in a slow nod. "I see. Are

you the girl from Vermont? Young Rodriguez mentioned you might come in." His voice was kind, and Molly relaxed a little.

"I'm Molly O'Connor," she said, shaking his hand.

"And I'm Blair."

Molly had almost forgotten about her stepmother. She turned to explain, but Blair was rummaging in her bag. "I think I'll take a few pictures. I'll be on Main Street." She left some money on the counter and was out the door before Molly could stop her.

"Should I come back later?" Molly asked.

Sam Fry looked down the length of the diner. Steam rose gently from coffee mugs, and the few customers were reading newspapers or looking out the windows toward the street. "Now's as good a time as any," he said. He motioned to the waitress. "Dot, you make the next breakfast. Me and Miss O'Connor here, we need to have a little chat." He unlatched the wooden gate at the end of the counter, poured himself a cup of coffee, and pointed to an empty booth. Molly slid into the red vinyl seat across from him, waiting while he settled his wide frame. He took a slow sip of coffee. "Now—how can I help you?"

Molly didn't know where to start. "You wrote the articles about my mom's accident—" she began.

"That's right. I had a terrible week—it ended my short career as a reporter."

"Why?" Molly asked.

"Ponce was a friend of mine."

"Ponce?"

"The man who drove the truck. Everyone called him Ponce, like the explorer: Ponce de León. But his real name was Paul Leone."

Molly nodded, although she didn't understand.

"Ponce was my buddy," Sam was saying. "The editor sent me to the scene. Told me to write a story about the crash as if I didn't know the guy. I wasn't cut out for that sort of thing. I quit soon after and bought this diner."

Molly's head whirled. She couldn't tell if she were in the past, with her mother, or in the present, huddled in her own, tired skin. "So you went to—the place where it happened?" she blurted.

"Afraid so. If you don't mind, I'll spare you the details."

Molly closed her eyes a minute, trying to erase her own vision of the crash. When she looked up, his eyes were soft with kindness. Molly gathered her courage for the next question. "Mr. Fry—"

"Sam," he interrupted.

"Sam," she said awkwardly, "maybe I'm being nosy, but—"

"Not to me. Why do you think I run a diner? I'm a nosy fool."

Nosy but nice, Molly thought. She took a deep breath. "I wondered—about the man in the truck."

"Ponce? What about him?"

"Who was he?"

"Just a surveyor. An old coot." Sam Fry finished his coffee and glanced toward the counter. New customers had wandered in, and the waitress was breaking eggs into a bowl and beating them furiously. "Ponce knew every inch of the hills around here. Always wore a bright yellow hat, for his helpers to take a sighting on." He frowned and passed a hand softly over his head, as if hoping to find hair on his bare scalp. "Did you wonder why he was with your mother?"

Molly nodded. "When I read your article, I thought— I mean, I wondered, if he and my mom—"

"Good Lord!" Sam wiped his forehead with his apron, then reached over to squeeze her hand. "Of course—I can see why you'd take it that way. When I wrote that story, I never dreamed there'd be a child who'd read it someday. I bet it worried you sick." He kept his big, soft hand closed over Molly's, and she smiled. Something was clearing inside her, like the sky washed clean by rain.

"Now, you get rid of that idea about your mama, right away," he said firmly. "Only one reason for Ponce to do anything with a woman."

"What's that?" Molly's hands shook. She pulled a napkin from the black box on the table and began to twist it slowly.

"Curiosity, plain and simple. He was a confirmed bachelor. Avoided women. Not like me, there's nothing I'd rather do than sit and drink coffee with a pretty girl." He winked at Molly, then said quickly, "Don't worry— I'm just a tease. But Ponce now, he was a loner."

Molly felt a slow release begin inside her, inching

from her feet up toward her head, like sap rising in the maple trees during the spring thaw. "So why was he there?"

Before Sam could answer, Dot cleared her throat and beckoned to Sam from behind the counter. "Five minutes, I promise," he called, then turned back to Molly. "I've tried to piece it together for years. After the accident, I called your father, but he wouldn't give me the time of day. Not that I blamed him. Imagine! Calling someone who'd just lost his wife—I felt like a fool." He rubbed his head. "Did he think the same thing about your mother?"

"I'm afraid so."

Sam shaded his eyes a minute with his big hand. "If I'd only known—tell him I'm sorry, will you?"

"Of course," Molly said, and thought: If only I could give this man a hug!

"What was your mother looking for?" Sam asked.

"An old homestead, where an ancestor might have buried something—valuable."

He raised his eyebrows. " 'Valuable' means one thing out here." He mouthed the word "gold" and then said, with a smile, "Don't worry. The secret's safe, even with an old busybody like me. And I'm not like Ponce, poking around in the hills every weekend. If you ask me, surveying was just a cover. He was really a gold digger at heart."

"Maybe geology was my mom's cover," Molly said.

"One of *those*." Sam shook his head. "They say geologists are just prospectors with fancy degrees."

Molly smiled, remembering what Sadie had said. "My mom once told someone the same thing."

"Well, she must have been a smart woman to choose one of the only men in town who could help her find something. Ponce had a map of the hills printed inside his skull."

Sam stood up abruptly, easing his large hips from the bench, raised his eyes toward the roof of the diner, and waved his fist. "That's good, Ponce—dying on a treasure hunt!" he boomed, and Molly thought Paul Leone must have heard his friend. The few people in the diner jumped and turned to stare.

Sam ignored them. He reached into his pocket to pull out an old wallet, digging inside until his thick fingers found a snapshot. He held it in front of Molly. "Now tell me—does that look like a woman chaser to you?"

The photograph was creased and worn. Molly could just make out the profile of a grizzled face beneath a battered hat. The man was old; he wore glasses and was bent over an instrument.

"Know what he's doing?" Sam asked.

Molly nodded. "Using a surveyor's transit. My dad has one."

Sam took the picture back. "Looks like you inherited your mother's smarts," he said. "You're a lucky girl. And brave, too. I bet your dad's proud of you."

"Not really," Molly admitted, although she couldn't stop smiling. "He's mad, actually. He didn't want me to come."

"He'll feel different now, won't he?" Sam squinted at

her. "So what have you discovered about this ancestor of yours?"

"Well, we know she had her own homestead near here, soon after the Gold Rush."

"*She*—a woman?" Sam said. He returned to the counter, picked up his spatula, and pushed some home fries into a pile on the grill, talking over his shoulder. Molly followed him and perched on a stool.

"I found an old photograph at home," Molly said. "It shows Abigail Parker—that was her name—getting her land. She's standing next to a sign that says 'Kenton Mine.' Ever heard of that? We think it's on Kanaka Creek."

Sam poured coffee for a man at the end of the counter. "No, Ramon asked me the same thing. I know Kanaka Creek—it's at the bottom of a steep draw near Allegheny. It takes some doing to get in there." He picked up an old meal check and scrawled a name on the back. "Go to my friend Shorty at the hardware store. He might know the mine—he's a panner from way back. Tell him I sent you."

A clatter of dishes silenced the diner. Dot pulled a broom from the closet and began to sweep up broken pottery with quick, angry strokes.

Sam Fry winced. "When Dot's mad, it's time to start hopping. You come back and tell me what happens, won't you?" He wiped his hand and reached across to shake hers. "Lots of luck. I don't know if I helped you much."

"You have—more than anyone," Molly said fervently. "Thank you, Sam."

"I should thank you. It was always a mystery to me, why Ponce would do something foolish in bad weather. Now I know there was gold involved, it explains everything."

He winked, and opened his arms expansively as she went to the door. "Sorry, folks," he called to the waiting customers, "I couldn't resist such a beautiful girl—and from Ver-mont, too."

Molly hurried down the steps and stood in the parking lot, raising her face to the sky. *Dad*, she called out silently, hearing the ring of his name inside her head. *Dad, it was just an accident. A stupid, stupid accident. She only loved you.*

CHAPTER 21

By nine o'clock, Molly and Blair had showered, un-packed, and stocked their small kitchen with food. Back in town, Blair parked her car near Ramon's street and looked longingly up the hill. Then she grabbed her cameras from the backseat.

"Sorry, Mol, but this is who I am: a photographer and a tourist."

"That's OK," Molly said, "you look more normal that way."

Blair laughed. She draped one camera over her shoulder while she held the other in front of her face to check the lens. "I guess you're right. I almost feel undressed without them. I'll just poke around here for a while—some of the details on the buildings are great."

Blair told Molly she would call Ramon's later, to check in. Molly put on her backpack and started down the street. Passing the ice-cream shop, she remembered the rack full of maps. She darted in and bought a detailed, Forest Service map of the area showing every river, stream, and dirt road. Molly zipped it into her backpack and walked slowly to Ramon's, wondering if he'd be glad to see her, or if he'd rather spend the day with Larry.

But Ramon was already outside his house, juggling a soccer ball from one knee to the other as he watched her come down the sidewalk. "Hey," he called. He kicked the ball across the yard and sauntered toward her. "What's the plan?"

She told him quickly about her breakfast at the diner. He grinned as she shared Sam's description of Paul Leone. "That must be a relief," he said.

"It sure is." Molly felt as if her face might split—she couldn't stop smiling. She found the crumpled piece of paper in her pocket. "Sam Fry told me that a man named Shorty, at the hardware store, might know where to find the Kenton Mine."

Ramon clapped her on the shoulder. "So what are we waiting for? Jewel's Hardware is just up the street."

Inside the dusty store, they found Shorty Adams, a short, plump man with round glasses. He told them the Kenton Mine was now a seedy motel with tourist cabins. "Got your panning gear?" he asked, as he penciled directions onto Molly's map. When Molly shook her head, he directed her to a low shelf, where tin pans of different depths and sizes were nestled inside one another. Molly bought an inexpensive pan, about fourteen inches wide, and tucked it under her arm. Outside

on the street, she grabbed Ramon's elbow. "Ramon—
this is wonderful! Don't you realize what this means—by
tomorrow night, we might see where Abigail lived. We
might even find the gold."

"Whatever you say." Ramon grinned. "I like it when
you get excited."

But Molly was already jogging down the sidewalk
ahead of him. "Come on!" she called. "We've got lots to
do."

They spent the rest of the morning planning the next
day's trip. They went to the store for cold cuts and
cheese to make sandwiches. Then Ramon gathered his
tools: shovels, a pick, gloves, and another tin pan. It was
battered and enormous, like a giant's soup bowl. "You
can see this one's been well used," he said. In the
afternoon, he took Molly to the river and they sat in the
sun, talking. Afterward, Molly couldn't believe she'd
only met him yesterday—he seemed like an old friend,
and she found herself laughing with him until her sides
ached.

Molly invited Ramon to dinner at their cabin. While
they sat on their tiny porch, eating dripping ears of corn,
Ramon told them about his school, what it was like to
grow up speaking two languages; how he hid his knowl-
edge of Spanish from his friends—"except for Larry. He
knows everything about me." While he talked, his leg
bounced, and as soon as he finished eating, he was on his
feet, scratching his back against a post like a horse in a
barn.

When Blair went inside, Molly giggled. "Don't you ever stop moving?"

Ramon plopped down beside her and ran his hands over his legs until the dark hair stood up like fur. "Sure. When I'm really impressed by something." He looked up at her, winked, and then froze, staring until Molly's face was hot.

Molly slept fitfully that night, and was dressed and waiting when Blair stumbled out of bed at six the next morning. She ate a piece of toast, but left her cereal to swell in the bowl, too nervous to finish it. As they drove along the empty main street, Molly said, "Blair—could you stop at the diner? I need to ask Sam something."

"Sure—but I doubt it's open this early." However, when Blair drew up in front of the silver restaurant, the lights were on inside and a lonely car, an enormous old Buick with tail fins, sat in the parking lot.

"Can you wait here?" Molly grabbed her pack and ran inside. If Sam Fry was surprised to see her, he didn't show it. Instead, he answered her question with a sober face, jotted a note on a paper napkin, and wished her luck. When she climbed back in the car, Blair gave her a questioning look, but didn't say anything, and Molly was grateful for her silence.

Ramon was waiting at the curb outside his house, shifting nervously from one foot to the other. Blair opened the trunk so he could stow his tools. "I brought lemonade," he said, holding up a big red jug. "Rosa said we'd need it today."

Blair thanked him and glanced at Molly. "Aren't you going to say good morning?"

"Oh, yeah. Sorry," Molly said. She smiled at Ramon, but inside she felt weak and slightly sick. Ramon nodded and climbed into the backseat.

For the first half hour or so, Blair tried to draw them into conversation. But when they rounded a sharp bend and saw the fast-moving, rocky bed of the Yuba River below, a heavy silence fell over the car. Molly opened the Forest Service map and searched the green-and-white-checked paper for Shorty's penciled marks. Outside the small town of North San Juan, they found the turn onto a narrow paved road to Allegheny. Blair checked the odometer. "Ten miles to the mine?" she asked cheerfully.

She drove carefully, concentrating on the sharp curves, while Molly watched the numbers inch slowly forward. It took forever for each tenth of a mile to click into place on the dashboard. Molly pulled the paper napkin from her pocket and twisted it between her fingers. When the gauge read 6.3, she whispered, "Blair, slow down." They passed a ranch on the right and then suddenly came upon a hairpin turn with no guardrail. Blair slowed, but kept driving.

"Wait, Blair!" Molly cried. She rolled down the window and gasped for air. "Blair, stop!"

"Here, hon? But we've only gone six miles—"

"Please," Molly begged.

Blair checked the rearview mirror and pulled over a hundred yards beyond the curve, where the road straightened. She looked at Molly, who sat frozen in her seat. "Is this the mine? I thought it was further. And I don't see any signs."

"We're not there yet," Molly said.

Blair bit her lip. "Oh," she whispered, suddenly understanding. "I see." She reached across to touch her, but Molly was on her way out of the car. She walked back along the edge of the road in the grass. In a minute, she heard the car doors slam, and turned to see Ramon and Blair, following in single file behind her.

There was nothing on the curve to indicate anything had ever happened there. After all, Molly thought, looking over the bank at the sparse weeds growing up through the gravel, it has been ten years.

She stood still a moment, feeling nothing, and then, without knowing what she was doing, scrambled down the bank, losing her footing in the loose gravel, sending a cascade of stones in front of her. She glanced back. Ramon and Blair were frozen above her, silhouetted against the sharp blue of the sky. Molly found what she wanted—a large, flat stone. She hauled it up the bank, starting another small landslide as she climbed, and set it at the edge of the highway, about six feet from the pavement.

"Molly, what—" Blair began, but Ramon understood. Without saying anything, he followed Molly down the hill, his sneakers slipping. He hauled another heavy rock up the steep pitch and set it beside the first one. Blair joined them for the next trip down. They fell and staggered, grabbing at tiny trees and bushes until their palms were scratched. Molly scraped her knee, but she didn't notice. She was lost in something that had no thoughts, words, or feelings to it. She went farther down the bank each time, bringing back bigger rocks, dragging them to the top of the hill.

The mound of stones grew; the sun was hot and their faces were streaked with dirt. Molly's arms ached. Finally, as they staggered to the road and dumped a last load, Molly said, "That's enough."

A car slowed on the highway. Its passengers turned to stare at them, their faces like empty dinner plates in the windows. Molly ignored them, as she ignored everything. Blair and Ramon stepped aside, waiting for instructions, but Molly forgot they were there. She was piling the stones carefully, making a tower—no, a cairn, Molly thought, thinking of the rocky piles that marked the mountain summits near home. She set the stones carefully, one on top of the other, choosing each by eye and feel. The tower seemed to build itself as if the stones knew where Molly wanted them to be, as if they'd been scattered and rolled on this bank for centuries, waiting for someone to bring them together.

When the tower was nearly waist height, Molly set a small stone on top and stepped back. The cairn was steady, though jumbled. Inside her head, Molly heard Todd's voice, from months before: *She was interested in geology, I guess.*

Molly stood there, feeling empty. She turned around. Ramon had crossed the highway; he sat in the grass on the far side, with his arms wrapped around his legs, as if to keep them still. Molly couldn't read what was in his face; he had covered his eyes with dark glasses. Blair was also motionless. Her hands dangled at her sides and tears ran down her cheeks.

"Molly," Blair whispered, "I think you're amazing."

Molly smiled. She had dreaded this moment. But it wasn't as awful as she'd expected. She felt like her small tower of stones: a little precarious, but sturdy.

"Blair, can you do something for me?"

"Anything."

"Take a picture, for Todd."

Blair winced, her green eyes darkening. "Now you ask me—but of course. I'll be right back." She disappeared around the bend.

Molly stood beside the cairn, listening for her mother, waiting for something to speak to her. A hot wind crackled in the trees at the foot of the ravine. Farther away, a truck growled, downshifting on a hill. Ramon crossed the road and stood staring at her.

"I'm OK," Molly said, as if he had asked. "I thought this would be weird, but it isn't. She's not here. She's home, in Vermont."

Ramon took off his sunglasses. His black eyes were shining. Without saying anything, he hugged her quickly, his body tense and hard against her. Molly trembled, and Ramon let go as Blair reappeared with her camera.

"How do you want me to do this?" Blair asked. Molly heard her voice quiver, even though she knew Blair was trying to be professional.

"A few pictures of the marker by itself," Molly said. "Some with me beside it and some from a distance, so you can see the trees in the background."

When it was time for Molly to stand quietly by the monument, she felt detached. She could imagine what Blair saw when she honed in on Molly with the lens: a thin, bony girl with her hair whipping across her face, her knees scraped below her shorts, her T-shirt streaked and wrinkled. Molly gazed steadily at the camera, imagining Blair's steady eye opening wide behind the lens. When the shutter clicked, Molly walked straight toward Blair and hugged her, with the sharp edges of the camera between them.

"Thanks," Molly said quietly. "Thanks for being here with me. Thanks for everything."

CHAPTER 22

When Molly opened the front door of the car, Blair suggested she join Ramon in the back. "I'll play chauffeur for a while," she said.

So Molly climbed in next to Ramon. Her body slowly came back to life. Her skin prickled with the heat and her legs throbbed from the work of heaving the stones.

"Listen, there's one thing you haven't seen yet." Molly rummaged in her pack for the daguerreotype. "Here's the woman who wrote the letters. Abigail Parker."

Ramon inched closer on the seat to peer over her shoulder. "So that's your ancestor," he said. "She looks like you."

Blair nodded from the front. "I think so, too."

"Let's see her letter again," he said, "the one about the gold." Molly spread the photocopy open across her knees, and Ramon took her hand, holding it under the shield of the paper. He grinned at her, tipping his head in a gesture that made her think of Kai.

"So we go down the hill, pace out four hundred yards, and we're there," he said casually.

Molly laughed. "You think there'll be a sign saying, 'Dig here'?" Ramon was distracting her; his fingers opened and closed in a gentle caress, tickling her palm. Molly felt hot, inside and out. She shifted on the seat and glanced toward Blair, who caught her eyes in the rearview mirror.

"We're at ten miles," Blair said. "Can you keep watch?"

Molly was relieved to pull her hand away and scan the highway. Around the next bend, they found the sign, dangling from a tree: KENTON MINE: CAMP AND CABINS. A dirt road veered off to the right and dropped into a ravine.

"Whew—this is some hill," Blair said, as the car crawled down the grade, following the switchbacks. There was no guardrail to keep them from plunging into the canyon. Blair's knuckles tightened on the wheel as the tires hit washboard and sent stones pinging against the rims. "I wouldn't like to drive this road in the winter," she said grimly.

At last they drew close to the bottom of the ravine, and after another three switchbacks, drove up a narrow valley ending in a wall of mountains. The road wound through trees and came to a halt beside a jumble of small cabins. The creek, a dry trickle, moved slowly through high, tumbled boulders.

Ramon jumped out and grabbed the tools. "Ready?"

Molly was staring at the rubble, piled in every direction on the riverbanks. "Was there an earthquake here?" she asked.

"It's all from mining," Ramon answered. "My dad told me sometimes they'd do so much dredging, they'd push the river aside."

Molly tried to imagine picking up Rock River, shifting the water into their pasture. She looked at Kanaka Creek. Stones were piled three feet deep on the near bank; the rubble stretched downstream beyond the bend in the river.

The sun slipped behind a cloud. Molly felt locked in, with the mountains looming over them, the pines rising in dark rows, and every inch of ground scoured by people who were gone. Blair suggested they have a snack by the water, and Molly followed without speaking. While Blair and Ramon ate muffins and talked, Molly stared at her stepmother. Something tugged at her, something so strong it made her stop and hold her breath. It wasn't a thought, but a feeling that slipped away like smoke before she could name it.

"You all right, Mol?" Blair asked.

Molly jumped up. "We'll never find anything here," she said. "It looks like a war zone."

Ramon took a sip of lemonade. "Don't give up yet— we haven't even started to look. If there's an old apple tree, it will stick out, with all these pines. And we can always pan for gold."

They finished eating in silence. Blair leaned back against a tree, in the shade. "This is peaceful—I'm going to rest here awhile," she said. "Which way are you going?"

Molly pulled Abigail's letter from her pack. " *'The creek makes a wide curve . . . Our cabin is about 400 yards downstream, where the land opens up a little,' "* she read, for the hundredth time.

Blair looked at her watch. "Let's plan to meet up here for lunch in a few hours—or I'll come find you." She closed her eyes.

"Four hundred yards is about a quarter mile," Molly said, picking up the shovel. "How will we measure it?"

"We'll guess," Ramon said. He took the pick and they started downstream, away from the cabins.

"These are called tailings," Ramon explained, as they picked their way over the loose heaps of stone.

Molly didn't answer. Her thoughts were still back on the highway where her mother had died. They passed a few rundown cabins, then followed the stream into the woods, where the banks began to look more normal again: overgrown with weeds and brush.

"The creek moves faster here," Ramon said. "The gold wouldn't settle—it likes a flat place, or a curve, away from the current."

"How do you know all this?" Molly asked.

"My dad. Sometimes, on weekends, we go panning." Ramon glanced over his shoulder. "We never find anything—just fool's gold, sometimes a little gold dust."

They entered deep woods. The pines were tall and the ground beneath them was rocky and bare. It was slow going, and they'd walked for a while before they realized they were a long way from the stream. "Maybe that's the wide curve Abigail talks about," Molly said. They listened for the creek's soft trickle and wound back through the trees to the bank where they found the streambed pulled into an enormous half-circle. "At home, we call this an oxbow," Molly said.

She looked around. The trees were enormous, almost menacing. "There's no clearing," she said. "I guess everything's all grown up. How will we find the apple tree?"

"We could sweep the area," Ramon said. He pointed away from the water. "They must have built on the flat, between the water and the hill. Let's put the tools here on the bank—then we'll know where we started." He spread his arms wide, until his body made a *T*. Molly did the same. When his fingertips grazed her own, she felt a chill along her spine, like fingers rippling over a keyboard.

Ramon grinned. "Now, let's spread out," he said. "We'll walk at the same pace."

Molly stepped sideways, and they began to crisscross the area, moving slowly from the river to the hill and back again until Molly thought they'd seen every pine tree twice. "Everything looks the same," she complained. There wasn't much underbrush, but the lower branches of the smaller trees whipped across her bare legs, leaving them scratched and bleeding. On the fourth or fifth trip through the woods, Molly had to go to the bathroom. She sent Ramon ahead, and waited until she was sure he was out of sight. Then she crouched behind a tree and when she stood up, the sunlight glinted on something round and smooth, just beyond the pine boughs. Molly snapped her shorts and parted the branches.

"Ramon!" she called.

Just ahead, in a tiny clearing, was an old, gnarled tree, one limb bent to the ground with age, its heart opened up like a giant clamshell. It was still alive. A sprinkling of wizened green apples dotted the branches like Christmas ornaments.

Ramon broke through the branches beside her. "Think we found it?"

Molly nodded and tiptoed into the open, looking over her shoulder as if Abigail's ghost might be following them. This place didn't have the lonesome feel of the highway. It was warm and cozy in the sunlight, with the sound of the river in the background.

Ramon was poking around in the long grass near the apple tree. "Someone lived here all right. Look at this." He pulled at an old timber, then held up a twisted piece of iron. His eyes lit with excitement, and one foot tapped the ground. "Let's start digging," he said.

"Where?" Molly said, but she was kneeling under the tree, scrabbling at the hard ground with her hands before he even answered her question.

Ramon laughed. "We brought tools, remember?" He

went back to the creek to get them. Soon, metal rang out against stone; they kicked rocks aside and pulled at the grass with their hands, finding gaps between the roots.

They worked for an hour or more until the small clearing was pockmarked with holes. Molly tossed her hair back from her face, then jammed her shovel into the ground so hard that she severed a small root. "Sorry, tree," she said impulsively, and then reddened.

"You talk to things?" Ramon asked.

Molly nodded, starting a new hole. "Sometimes. Weird, huh?"

"Not really. I do that too, actually. I just don't admit it to most people."

Molly tossed dry earth and loose stones to the side. "Like what—what do you talk to?"

"Mostly animals. But other things, too." Ramon glanced at her. "Promise you won't laugh?"

"Of course I won't."

"Well, I talk to a tree in my yard."

"Really? What do you tell it?"

"Secrets," Ramon said. "Know what I mean?"

"Yeah." Molly thought of her river. "I know just what you mean."

They returned to their digging. Even under the trees, the sun was hot. Sweat trickled down Molly's back, and her arms were streaked with dirt. "This is silly," she said after a while. "We could be here all day—maybe someone found it years ago."

She grunted and jabbed the ground, starting a new hole. Her shovel rang out like a gong. "What was *that?*"

She dropped to her knees and scraped away the dirt with her bare hands. In a moment, something sharp and square appeared. They brushed the dry soil away gently until they could see a dark piece of metal. Ramon slipped a stick down beside it and pried the box from its hole. He set it on the grass near Molly's knees and they stared at it a moment, keeping their distance as if it held a bomb.

It was a dented, metal box about eight inches square. Molly's hands shook as she tugged at the rusted fastening, trying to loosen it. It was crusted tight with age. Ramon opened his jackknife and wiggled the latch with the leather punch. When he'd worked it free, Molly lifted the lid, holding her breath. Inside was a small book, brittle and moldy with age, a packet of letters tied with ribbon, and a tiny cloth sack.

Molly wiped her hands on her shorts before picking up the leather book. The cover was damp with mold. She wiped it with the end of her shirt, then opened it. Inside, on the flyleaf, was a signature in familiar handwriting: "*Abigail Parker. 1850. Being an account of my journey across the country, and all the rivers we crossed.*"

Molly's heart was beating fast. She skimmed the first few pages. Each had a heading with the name of a river: *The Missouri. The Kansas. The Platte.* "Look, Ramon," Molly said, "it's a diary. It tells about Abigail's trip west."

Ramon rocked back and forth on his heels. "Aren't you going to open the bag?" he asked eagerly. He was holding the soft pouch gingerly, as if it were made of cobwebs.

Molly picked it up. Something rattled inside. "Oh, Ramon, do you think—?" She untied the drawstring, slipped her hand inside, and felt a cluster of tiny stones. She pulled out the biggest lump: a soft, honey-colored rock the size of a robin's egg.

"Looks like gold to me," Ramon said.

Molly opened her palm to the sunlight. Tiny gold flecks, soft as talcum powder, clung to her fingers. She brushed the dust carefully back into the bag and stood up, clutching the pouch in her fist. She had heard Blair's voice calling their names. The pines blurred as Molly blinked away tears.

Branches snapped and Blair emerged from the woods, squinting in the bright sunlight. She looked small and worried; her dark hair was pulled back from her face. When she saw Molly, she opened her mouth to speak but closed it quickly.

Molly held up the bag, then pointed to the box. Her voice was frozen in her throat.

"We found the gold," Ramon called, and his words seemed to float in the sunlight. When he saw Molly's tears, he turned away and began to shovel dirt back into the holes at the base of the tree.

"Dear heart," Blair said, hurrying to Molly, "did something go wrong?"

"No," Molly said. She swallowed hard and pulled herself up straight, looking into Blair's green eyes. The misty feeling had become something she could name.

"It's just—" She gulped, trying to control herself, then gave up. "I was thinking how I wished my mother were still alive. But then I thought if she were here, I wouldn't have met Ramon. And I wouldn't know you. And I love you," she cried, sobbing now.

"I love you too," Blair said, stroking Molly's hair.

They stood there for a long moment, holding each other, while the sun's warmth beat down on their shoulders and the rhythmic thud of Ramon's shovel filled the silence in the clearing.

CHAPTER 23

The next week passed in a rush. At Rosa's insistence, Molly and Blair left their motel and moved onto the Rodriguez's screened porch where they fell asleep each night to small-town noises: cats yowling, televisions humming, the hollow tap of steps on the sidewalk. Every morning, they went to breakfast at Pauline's. By the third day, Sam Fry was preparing their orders when they arrived. Then Blair would wander off to take photographs. Sam had introduced her to some people he called "The *real* old-timers—not young upstarts like me." Blair slipped quietly into their lives with her camera, and talked with excitement about a series called "portraits from the gold country."

Molly went to the Historical Society with Ramon, and helped him mow the lawn, sweep the porch, and keep watch when the building was open to the public. Later,

Larry joined them for walks along the Yuba River. When they left the town behind, Ramon showed Molly how to pan for gold, how to scoop water, mud, and stones from a quiet place near the bank and loosen the pebbles from the clay; swirling, shaking, and sifting until there was nothing left in the pan but a fine, black grit. Molly didn't care if she found anything, but she liked the way the pan and her hands made a noisy dance above the water. Once in a while, Ramon would whoop and call out: "We struck pay dirt!" And he'd point proudly to tiny golden flecks settling in the bottom of the pan. Molly came home sunburned and blissfully tired every night.

After dinner, sitting at the kitchen table with Ramon's sisters hanging over her shoulders and the dishes pushed aside, Molly read aloud from the diary. She followed Abigail Parker's family across the plains, over the Rockies, into the desert, and across the Sierras to Kanaka Creek. The entries were quick, but telling: "*Swam in the Vermilion River in my chemise*," Abigail wrote. "*I hope Matthew wasn't watching.*" The Rodriguez girls had fun guessing at the relationships until, on the last night, when Molly read about the family reaching Kanaka Creek, Christine (the youngest sister) cried, "But what happened? Did Abigail marry Matthew?"

Molly smiled. "She did. And they had a little girl named Molly."

"Was that *you?*" Christine cried, and everyone laughed.

"No—she was my ancestor," Molly said. And she

continued the story as she had pieced it together. The girls' eyes grew round as Molly told them about her ancestors who moved back east to Vermont, about Grand Nan and Sadie (their descendants) who lived on adjoining farms and wouldn't speak to each other. She told them how Ashley O'Connor had written the Historical Society asking a simple question about her ancestors—and received a surprising answer. As she talked, she could feel Abigail Parker at her back, smiling with her at the dark eyes around the table.

Rosa Rodriguez laughed. "Molly, you're a born storyteller."

Molly hugged her arms across her chest, feeling warm and surprised. Something had changed inside her, she realized, though she didn't know how to name it.

Later, Molly lay on her cot, still dressed in her shorts and T-shirt, and listened to Blair's steady breathing. She was too excited to sleep. And she was nervous about seeing her father. They'd talked once on the phone, but all she'd told him was that everything was fine, and she'd explain when she saw him. What would he think?

Something snapped outside and a familiar shadow slid past. Molly crept to the end of the porch.

"Ramon?" she whispered.

He rose from the bushes, pressed his face to the screen, and gestured to her. "Come here a minute."

Molly raised the latch gently and slipped out under the trees. The streetlamps cast deep shadows across the grass. She let Ramon take her hand and lead her behind the house. They walked slowly; the ground was cool and dry under Molly's toes. Ramon drew her down beside him on a wooden bench at the end of the yard.

"I wanted to say good-bye tonight," he whispered. "When no one was around."

Molly peered into his face. Her eyes were growing accustomed to the dark. His smile, like his shirt, was a dusky white among the shadows. "I can't believe I've only known you a week," she said softly.

Ramon swatted at a moth as it flew past her ear, then let his arm settle casually around her shoulders. "It's been more than a week, really, if you count all those phone calls," he said, and then laughed. "I wonder what Miss Darby will say when she gets the bill. I may have to turn over all of this month's salary."

"You should take half the gold. After all, you helped me find it."

Ramon shook his head. "No thanks. It's yours. Anyway, I don't want Abigail to put a hex on me."

"She wouldn't do that," Molly laughed. They were quiet a minute. A lone car swept its lights slowly down the street and disappeared.

"Will you write me?" Ramon asked softly.

"Of course," Molly said.

"You won't forget me?"

Molly clapped a hand over her mouth to stifle her laughter. "How could I forget you?" She turned so she could see his face, full on, and smiled.

"Listen." Ramon's knee began its jiggling bounce. He jumped up, forgetting to whisper. "I'll come visit you this winter, if I can save up the money. You'll teach me to ski. It's like this, right?" He bent his knees and started to swing his body from side to side with his feet locked together and his arms flailing. He fell sideways onto the grass.

"Right," Molly laughed. "Perfect form." Molly didn't want this to end, ever. She wondered if she'd cry when she got on the plane. What if she never saw Ramon again?

Ramon flopped on his back. The streetlight in the alley cast a dappled yellow light across his face. "Think your brother will like me?"

"Sure," Molly said, though she didn't know what Todd would say. Suddenly she realized that it didn't matter what Todd thought of Ramon, what anyone thought of him, for that matter. She had found him for herself.

Ramon clambered back up onto the bench. They talked and talked, forgetting the time, forgetting to keep their voices low. Molly found herself repeating one of her father's Irish stories, and Ramon laughed out loud. A light snapped on upstairs and Ramon's father appeared, a dark silhouette behind the gauze curtain.

"Who's there?" he called softly.

Molly cringed, but Ramon hurried to the house and peered up at the window. "It's OK, Dad. Molly and I were just talking."

Mr. Rodriguez passed his hand over his face, as if washing it. "Well, make sure that's *all* you do. I think you'd better get to bed now," he said gruffly, and flicked off the light.

"We got off easy that time," Ramon said. "Luckily, he likes you."

Molly followed him to the back door. Ramon paused on the steps and grinned down at her. The outside light made a spotlight over his dark hair. "Well?" he said, tapping his foot.

"Well, what?" Molly said.

"Here I am at my door on our last date. Aren't you going to kiss me good night?"

Molly hesitated. Would he know she'd never kissed a boy before? But there was no time to think. Ramon's lips were soft and prying as he stepped down and wrapped his arms around her. Molly was surprised by the flick of his tongue in her mouth and the press of his legs against her. "Kiss me back," Ramon whispered, and Molly did, her lips fluttering softly at first, then searching for his warm, salty taste. Little waves of hot and cold raced along her back and into her legs.

Ramon pulled away suddenly, turned a cartwheel in the grass, then bounded onto his hands and walked over to Molly with his feet waving in the air.

"I've flipped over you," he said.

Molly leaned against the kitchen door. She felt limp, as if the heat pulsing in her belly had drained all her limbs. Ramon feels this way about me? Molly O'Connor?

Ramon was showing off now. He tumbled from a somersault into a flip and landed on his feet with a bounce, throwing his arms wide for her applause. When Molly clapped her hands, the upstairs light snapped on again, making a square yellow swath across the concrete patio. Rosa Rodriguez's voice seemed to ripple toward them.

"Ramon—didn't you hear your father?"

"OK, Rosa," Ramon said, "we're coming in now."

They went inside. Ramon turned on the light and went to the refrigerator. "Want a glass of milk?" he asked.

Molly nodded. As he poured, she whispered, "Ramon—imagine if you'd never written my father."

"I started this whole thing, didn't I? Did you ever wish I hadn't?"

"Sometimes," Molly admitted. "But not now." She drank her milk, feeling its cool comfort slide down her throat. "You'll never know how glad I am."

"Oh, yes I do. You just showed me," Ramon said. He looked away, and Molly felt shy, too. Before she could say anything else, Ramon snapped off the light, then came to find her. He put his arms around her and kissed her again. "It's nicer in the dark," he whispered. Molly agreed, but she couldn't answer. Not with her mouth on his.

Coming up the skyway in Boston the next afternoon, Molly caught sight of her father's square figure, pressed close to the glass. He was scanning the passengers as they walked up the ramp and Molly could tell, from the way he tugged nervously at his mustache, that he was worried. She darted through the crowd, dropped her pack on the floor, and threw her arms around him. Mark O'Connor stumbled backward, then caught his balance.

"Hey, Molly." He laughed and tugged her hair, then held her at arm's length. "You look great. How was it?"

"Wonderful," Molly said. "I can't wait to tell you."

His smile deepened, but his eyes left her as Blair came up beside them and put her bags down. They kissed so long and deep that Molly turned away. Did Ramon and I look like that? she wondered. So moony and wet-eyed? The thought of Ramon's embrace brought a hot tug to her belly. "Come on, you guys," Molly blurted, "you're embarrassing me."

Blair pulled her head back but kept her arms on Mark's shoulders. "Watching you and Ramon made me miss your dad," she said.

Molly's father raised his eyebrows. "I hope he behaved himself."

Blair squeezed her husband's arm. "Don't worry, he's a nice boy—and funny."

Molly followed her parents down the escalator, half listening to Blair as she chattered about their stay with Ramon's family. She felt jittery and unsettled. When they reached the carousels, Blair went to find a bathroom. Suitcases tumbled onto the moving conveyer belt, and Molly's father pulled her away from the crowd. "Let's get this over with," he said hoarsely. "What did you find?" His eyes were wary.

"It's all right, Dad. I promise." Molly told him about Sam and his diner, about the surveyor everyone called Ponce, the man who avoided women, but joined Ashley because he wanted to help her. "I saw his picture," Molly said. "He was an *old* guy."

Her father's expression softened. "You mean old, like me?"

"No, Dad. I mean old like Sadie, or Grand Nan. He was a retired surveyor. Sort of ugly. With a grizzled beard and a beat-up hat." Molly stuck out her chin and squinted her eyes, imitating the photo Sam carried in his wallet. Her father still looked puzzled, as though she spoke a foreign language.

"Dad, don't you see? He wasn't a boyfriend."

"What was he, then?" Her father's voice cracked, like Todd's when it first started its downward plunge.

"Mommy really was looking for gold, just like I thought." Molly spoke faster, and she gripped his arm. "She needed someone to help her find the mine. This man, Paul Leone, knew the mountains—" Molly caught her breath. Was her father crying? One side of his face was twisted, as if he'd been stung, and his cheeks were wet. He rubbed his eyes and went to the windows, away from the crowd. Molly followed him, standing off to the side. Why wasn't he happy with her news?

"What a fool I've been," he said at last. "All these years, I thought the worst of her. And I blamed myself, for trying to keep her home."

"But you didn't," Molly said.

"Didn't what?" he asked. His voice was slow, as if he were half asleep.

"You didn't keep her home. She did what she wanted."

This time, a light seemed to come on in his face, and he sat down suddenly in the row of plastic seats, as if her words had pushed him over. He laughed, a hard, dry noise, then looked up at her. "For a smart man, I'm pretty slow, aren't I?" He tapped his forehead, then frowned. "Molly, I'm not saying I don't believe you— but why wouldn't she tell me about the gold before she left?"

Molly grasped for the woman she'd tried to find, the woman whose spirit was like quicksilver scuttling across the floor. "She wanted to surprise you," Molly said.

"Now, how do you know that?" But he didn't seem to want an answer. He pulled out a handkerchief and blew his nose. Molly shifted her pack to her other shoulder.

"That's something I forgot about her," he said. "She'd discover something, and keep it inside, worry it over, test out all the angles, until she knew she was right. Then it would burst out, like an explosion."

He stood up and linked his arm in hers. "I'm so used to thinking of what she did to me, at the end—I've lost who she was. Poor Ashley." His eyes were red again. "I wish I could tell her I'm sorry."

"Maybe she knows," Molly whispered.

Her father's mouth twisted into a half smile. He looked out the window, past the planes taxiing down the steamy runway. "Love Minus Zero," he said.

Molly stared at him as if he'd lost his mind. "Dad— what are you talking about?"

He tugged his mustache. "It's a Bob Dylan song—she played it all the time. I should have paid attention to the words."

"How does it go?" Molly asked.

To her surprise, her father put his hands on his hips and sang, his voice tentative at first, then slowly growing full and strong. An older woman standing nearby edged away, but he didn't seem to notice.

" *'My love, she speaks like silence,'* " he sang. " *'Without ideals or violence. She doesn't have to say she's faithful, but she's true, like ice, like fire.'* "

Molly recognized the tune; she and Kai sometimes played old Dylan albums at the Stewarts' house. "Go on," she said.

Her father shook his head. "That's all I remember. She was as faithful as the woman in the song, but I didn't see it." He cleared his throat. "Your mother was a complicated lady, like the rocks she studied. She always said the roughest, most unlikely stone could have a jewel hidden inside." His cheeks were wet, but he let the tears run. "I didn't see what a gem she was, until it was too late." He passed his hand lightly over Molly's head. "Luckily, she left two precious stones behind for me— you and Todd."

Molly's face burned as she followed her father back to the baggage area. *Like ice, like fire.* Molly thought of the cold, lonely years, now behind her, when the memories of her mother were frozen, locked in an icy grip by her family's silence. This summer it seemed as if everything had thawed and melted, until now, images of her mother flickered and rose, like dancing flames fed by a wind. The fire surged in her heart. She wanted to run outside, to leap through the hot raindrops splattering on the runway, to shout above the roar of the planes.

Her father turned around and smiled. "You look happy."

Molly nodded. "I am. Say, Dad—"

But her father wasn't listening. He had caught sight of Blair, grabbing her suitcase as it rattled past on the conveyer. "There's the best thing that ever happened to me," he said. He dropped Molly's arm and pushed through the crowd. Molly stood on tiptoe to watch. Their two heads came together: Mark O'Connor's sandy hair above Blair's dark curls. Blair set her bag down as Molly's father whispered something in her ear and then, while people jostled past them, they embraced, oblivious to children crying and men calling out for taxis.

This time, Molly wasn't embarrassed. As if they were two children in her care, she retrieved their suitcases, stowed them on a cart, and took her father's arm.

"Come on," she said gently, "it's time to go home."

CHAPTER 24

Molly woke when their car made its final turn off the dirt road. As they rumbled across the bridge, she sat up, just in time to see the dark opening beneath the trees. *Hey, river,* she called silently, *I'm home.*

She checked her watch: nine o'clock, Vermont time. Their car crested the hill and drove into the yard. The house was ablaze with light; a string of balloons danced across the porch and a banner was draped over the railing. WELCOME BACK, GOLD MINERS! it said.

Molly rubbed her eyes. "What's going on?" she asked sleepily.

Her father shrugged. "Looks like some kind of party. Better get out and see."

Molly grabbed her pack and walked slowly up the steps, but before she could touch the door, Kai flung it open and dragged Molly in. "Surprise!" she cried. Molly stood in the doorway, stunned. Grand Nan sat in the rocker, her glasses slightly askew, her small feet barely grazing the floor. Sadie stood by the stove, stirring something, and Todd was perched on the kitchen counter, swinging his bare legs. "Cheers," he said, toasting Molly with his soda.

Molly couldn't move. "Grand Nan and Sadie in the same room?" she blurted.

Sadie nodded. "We decided it was all foolishness, didn't we, Beth?"

Grand Nan nodded and hoisted herself from the chair. As Molly hurried to kiss her grandmother's brittle cheek, everyone began talking and hugging each other. Even Sadie gave Molly a dry peck on the forehead.

"So you came back after all," she said.

Molly grinned, surprised at how easy it was to meet Sadie's steely gaze. "Did you think I wouldn't?" She took a deep breath. "Boy, it sure smells good in here. What's cooking?"

"Lasagna," said Todd. "Your favorite. Kai helped me bake it." He jumped off the counter and gave Molly a quick, sideways hug, then pointed sheepishly to the empty plate beside him. "There were hors d'oeuvres too, but we got hungry, didn't we, Grand Nan?"

"Did we eat them up?" Grand Nan gave Todd a worried look as she settled slowly into her rocker. "I'm afraid I don't remember."

Molly smiled. "It doesn't matter, Grand Nan."

Mark O'Connor disappeared into the pantry and

emerged carrying bottles of champagne, sparkling cider, and beer. "Molly, get out the best glasses," he said. "This is a night to celebrate."

Molly went into the den and opened the corner cupboard. She took out seven dusty glasses, rinsed them at the sink, and dried them. I'm home, she thought, looking around the room at her family. Was it all a dream? As she put the glasses on the table, set with a bright red cloth and their best blue dishes, she noticed a card propped against a candlestick. "Molly—Ramon called!" said the note.

Kai nudged Molly. "I talked to him," she whispered. "He sounds so-oo cute." She set the salad bowl on the table and murmured, "Are you in love?"

Molly nodded. How could she tell Kai she was in love with everyone right now? With Kai herself, her snapping black eyes reminding her of Ramon. With her father, sipping his beer and pinching Blair gently as she passed him. With Todd, his rusty hair sticking up every which way, and with Grand Nan, her soft, innocent smile following Molly. She could even say she loved Sadie, dumping hot beans into a serving dish as if the vegetable made her cross. And Blair—Molly caught her stepmother's eye and they shared a shy smile.

"Yeah," Molly said at last, "I'm in love, all right."

When they were seated at the table, Mark O'Connor stood at one end with the neck of the champagne bottle pointed toward the door. He cleared his throat. "We've got lots to celebrate tonight," he said. Everyone picked up their forks but he called, "Wait a minute. I'd like to propose a toast."

Todd groaned. "I'm going to pass out from hunger."

"Pass out, then," his father said. "First, I want to welcome our travelers home." He raised his glass to Molly, then Blair. "Second, I want to congratulate two old birds on their decision to start speaking again."

"Watch your language, young man," Sadie said in her peppery voice. She looked at Molly. "Your grandmother and I decided it was time to let the past sleep."

"A-men—I'll drink to that!" Molly's father cried, his voice breaking. He pressed the champagne cork, gently wiggling it. Molly held her breath until the cork burst from the bottle and ricocheted off the ceiling, landing in the salad. Kai squealed, everyone laughed, and then food was passed up the table, the bread basket made the rounds and Molly took long, luxurious bites from her lasagna.

Kai nudged her. "You're home just in time—tomorrow night's the last performance of *Midsummer Night's Dream.*"

Molly clutched her arm. "How could I forget to ask? Was it wonderful? I can't wait to see you."

"She's good," Todd said with emphasis.

Molly raised her eyebrows. "She must be sensational, if you think she's good." Todd kicked her under the table, but Molly ignored him. Nothing was going to bother her tonight, she decided. She smiled at Kai, and basked in the sweet smells from the table. It was hard to

believe she had started the summer feeling angry with
her best friend.

She tried a few sips of Blair's champagne, which made
her head feel light, then switched to sparkling cider. The
talk grew louder and in the midst of it, Kai asked Molly,
"So—did you find your mother?"

"Which one?" Molly asked lightly. "I found them
both."

The sounds at the table died, as if someone had slowly
twisted the volume knob on a radio. Kai shrank in her
chair, but Blair, who was sitting next to her, grabbed her
hand. "It's all right, sweetie," she said to Kai, then
looked at Molly, her eyes soft with pleasure. "Thanks,
Mol," she whispered. She opened her arms wide, as if to
embrace everyone. "Molly and I had a great trip. I know
she wants to tell you all about it, but first, I have to get
something."

Blair disappeared for a few minutes. When she came
back, the talk was rowdy again. Blair tapped her glass
and handed Molly a large package wrapped in brown
paper.

"I made this for you and Todd before we left," Blair
said. "But I saved it for our homecoming."

Molly glanced at Todd. "You open it," he said. She
tore off the wrapper, which covered a black leather
album. Todd stood up and looked over her shoulder as
Molly turned the pages. The pictures began with a
reprint of the daguerreotype, showing Abigail with her
shovel, and moved forward in time. Molly recognized
pictures she'd seen in her grandmother's albums, and

the snapshots of her mother that Sadie had hidden. There were photographs of Ashley as a young woman, of Molly and Todd as babies, of their family now.

Molly looked at Blair. "When did you do this?"

"I reshot a lot of pictures this summer. I didn't write any captions, because you know more about these people than I do. There's space at the end, for the pictures we took out west."

"Thank you, Blair." Molly stroked the embossed leather cover. "This is wonderful. And that reminds me. I have presents for everyone."

She found her backpack and rummaged inside for her small packages. The easiest one first, she thought, handing Kai a tiny box. Her friend pulled out a pair of dangling earrings, with sparkling silver stars at the end. "For the star of the show," Molly said.

Everyone groaned at her pun, and Molly laughed. She caught her father's eye. He was watching her with surprise, as though he hardly recognized his own daughter. Molly drew herself up tall, feeling bold and sure of herself. She gave her grandmother the river scrapbook— "a diary by your great-grandmother," she said, and added softly, "Tomorrow I'll come over, and we'll read it together. All right?"

"Why, thank you, Molly," Grand Nan said, and opened the book. She traced the words gently with her fingertips and a flush of pleasure spread across her face.

"It tells all about Abigail Parker's wagon trip," Molly said. "She had an exciting life." Molly took her grandmother's hand. "Just like Ashley."

When Molly bent over her pack again, Sadie's eyes glittered. "Don't worry, Cousin Sadie, there's something for you, too." Molly pulled out the small cloth sack, carefully spread a napkin and poured the tiny lumps of gold onto the cloth.

No one spoke, although Mark O'Connor whistled, and Sadie's face turned a soft pink. She picked up the biggest lump and rolled it between her thumb and forefinger like a marble. "Who would think," she said, clearing her throat, "that these small stones could cause such heartache?"

"Not just heartache," Molly whispered, although she couldn't explain what she felt inside. Dark and lost for over a hundred years, the secrets in these stones seemed as lustrous as spun honey, shot through with sunlight.

"I can't take these," Sadie said.

Molly laughed, relieved to hear the sharp tone return to the old woman's voice. "We'll share them, then," Molly said. "You and Todd and I."

Todd was handling the stones gingerly. "I feel bad, Mol—I should have believed you. Where'd you find them?"

Molly put her hands on the table and told them about the road winding down to the cabins, about the tailings on the riverbanks, and how she and Ramon dug holes beneath the old apple tree. She held up the box, which she had cleaned and scrubbed at Ramon's, and presented it to her father.

"It's not much," she said.

Her father turned it over, studying the old hinges, the

funny clasp. "What do you mean, not much? It's a treasure chest, and it survived the Gold Rush. Who knows what stories it could tell us." Then he added, his voice full of emotion. "Your mother would be proud of you, Mol. Now, don't you think you should tell Todd about the present you gave me at the airport?"

Molly took a deep breath and explained, for the second time that day, about Paul Leone, the surveyor. Todd didn't say anything, but his eyes grew soft and round with relief. Molly heard a little catch of breath behind her. When she turned around, Grand Nan was smiling bravely, but tears had collected on the rims of her glasses. Molly slipped her dinner napkin into her grandmother's lap. Grand Nan wiped her eyes, and Molly turned back to her brother.

"I brought you something, too," she said, placing a small envelope in his hands. He tore it open and stared at the color prints. One showed Molly standing beside the road; the other was the cairn, leaning at a slow angle toward the highway.

Todd frowned, then scratched his head. "What is this?" he asked hoarsely.

"That's where the truck—went off the road," Molly said carefully, feeling conscious of Grand Nan beside her. But her grandmother's eyes were vacant, and Molly knew she'd disappeared into her own cloudy world again.

"Who built the marker?" Todd asked.

"I did. Ramon and Blair helped me."

Molly glanced at her father. He was staring into space,

tugging his mustache. Sadie was sitting beside him, and the corners of her mouth trembled, threatening to pitch downward. "I didn't mean to dump cold water on the party," Molly said.

"You didn't." Blair pushed her chair back, stood up, and put her hand on Todd's shoulder. "If you ask me, there've been too many things we couldn't talk about around here. I think we should thank Molly for letting all the old bats fly out of the closet."

At the mention of bats, Grand Nan looked around nervously and put her hands to her hair. Everyone laughed, and Mark O'Connor leaped to his feet. "Open the windows! Sweep out the cobwebs! Let the breeze come in!" He flung the door open wide and brushed away the imaginary creatures with his hand.

Molly grinned. Everything was going to be all right. Absolutely everything.

"Here, here!" Todd shouted. He pounded the table with his fist. The crystal glasses jumped and one tipped over, spilling champagne on his grandmother. Everyone began to move. Grand Nan fumbled for her napkin, to wipe her skirt.

In the midst of the confusion, Blair called, "Wait! Hold everything! I want to take a picture. A portrait of the whole family."

Everyone groaned and Molly said, "Only if you're in it, too."

"Fine," Blair said, "I'll take a time exposure." She set the camera on a stool, squinted through the lens, and began to wave them into place. "Everyone gather around

Grand Nan, in the rocker. Todd, get closer to Molly. Come on, it's only this once. . . . That's right, Kai, you snuggle in on Todd's other side. . . . Mark, stop that whistling, and save a place for me. . . . Sadie, you can't hang out on the side. Get in the picture!" Blair waved her hands, her small body bent over the stool.

Molly felt her father's hand settle on her shoulder. She turned to smile into his eyes. They were ruddy with happiness. "You did this, Mol," he said. "You brought us together."

Molly beamed, and peered at her brother. Todd was grinning at Kai, who had nestled close beneath his shoulder. *Goof,* Molly thought and wished, with a pang, that Ramon's hand was in her own. She wanted him there beside her with his knee jouncing. She looked down at her grandmother. Grand Nan's small head was poised and still. Sadie, off to the side, was blinking furiously behind her glasses.

We *are* together, Molly thought, and suddenly felt her mother's presence, a light, loving spirit, alive and bold right in the middle of the portrait.

"Ready?" Blair called, checking the focus one last time. "Here we go—" She pressed the shutter and scrambled to join Molly's father.

"Piece of pizza!" Todd yelled, and everyone smiled as the camera whirred for a long moment, then clicked.

Molly saw the shutter close just before the flash spilled whirling purple circles into her eyes.

"Hold still," Blair cried. "Let me take another one." But the phone's sudden ring drowned their groans. Todd and Molly tripped over each other, leaping for it. "Beat you!" Molly cried, snatching the receiver and pushing Todd aside. "Hello?" she laughed, and then held her breath. When she heard a familiar voice, she gave Kai the thumbs-up sign.

"Hey, Ramon," she said. And his laugh sang out across the miles, as her family made its own discordant harmony in the background, filling the kitchen with the warmth of home.